USA TODAY Bestselling Author

# REBECCA YORK

### RUTH GLICK WRITING AS REBECCA YORK

# THE SECRET NIGHT

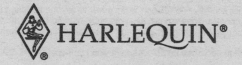

# HARLEQUIN®

TORONTO • NEW YORK • LONDON
AMSTERDAM • PARIS • SYDNEY • HAMBURG
STOCKHOLM • ATHENS • TOKYO • MILAN • MADRID
PRAGUE • WARSAW • BUDAPEST • AUCKLAND

ISBN 0-373-88686-1

THE SECRET NIGHT

Copyright © 2006 by Ruth Glick

# ABOUT THE AUTHOR

Award-winning, bestselling novelist Ruth Glick, who writes as Rebecca York, is the author of close to eighty books, including her popular 43 Light Street series for Harlequin Intrigue. Ruth says she has the best job in the world. Not only does she get paid for telling stories, he's also the author of twelve cookbooks. Ruth and her husband, Norman, travel frequently, researching locales for her novels and searching out new dishes for her cookbooks.

## Books by Rebecca York

HARLEQUIN INTRIGUE

143—LIFE LINE*
155—SHATTERED VOWS*
167—WHISPERS IN THE NIGHT*
179—ONLY SKIN DEEP*
188—BAYOU MOON
193—TRIAL BY FIRE*
213—HOPSCOTCH*
233—CRADLE AND ALL*
253—WHAT CHILD IS THIS?*
273—MIDNIGHT KISS*
289—TANGLED VOWS*
298—TALONS OF THE FALCON†
301—FLIGHT OF THE RAVEN†
305—IN SEARCH OF THE DOVE†
318—TILL DEATH US DO PART*
338—PRINCE OF TIME*
407—FOR YOUR EYES ONLY*
437—FATHER AND CHILD*
473—NOWHERE MAN*
500—SHATTERED LULLABY*
534—MIDNIGHT CALLER*
558—NEVER TOO LATE*

606—BAYOU BLOOD BROTHERS
        "Tyler"
625—THE MAN FROM TEXAS**
633—NEVER ALONE**
641—LASSITER'S LAW**
667—FROM THE SHADOWS*
684—GYPSY MAGIC
        "Alessandra"
706—PHANTOM LOVER*
717—INTIMATE STRANGERS*
745—THE BOYS IN BLUE
        "Jordan"
765—OUT OF NOWHERE*
783—UNDERCOVER ENCOUNTER
828—SPELLBOUND*
885—RILEY'S RETRIBUTION
912—THE SECRET NIGHT*

*43 Light Street
**43 Light Street/Mine To Keep
†Peregrine Connection

# CAST OF CHARACTERS

**Nicholas Vickers**—He had secrets to hide.

**Emma Birmingham**—She was desperate to save her sister's life.

**Damien Caldwell**—He used people for his own ends.

**Henry Briggs**—Damien Caldwell trusted him, but only so far.

**Trailblazer**—Why was he following Nicholas Vickers?

**Margaret Birmingham**—She'd gotten into a bad situation, and she couldn't get herself out.

**Butch McCard**—He made no secret of his hatred for Nicholas Vickers.

**Alex Shane**—Could Emma and Nick count on the Light Street detective?

# Chapter One

Nicholas Vickers, private investigator, was as comfortable in a graveyard as he was in his own game room. That the graveyard hadn't seen a new grave dug in a very long time only enhanced his sense of belonging.

Wrapping the night's shadows around himself like a cloak, he stood beneath a large maple tree and watched a biker gang enjoying the ambiance of Ten Oaks Cemetery. Their idea of fun did not include showing respect for the dead.

Eight of them had roared up on bikes half an hour ago. The two who'd brought girls with them had made use of the scant privacy afforded by a pair of chipped and listing headstones to satisfy their sexual needs. They were now relaxing with their friends, lounging among the tall grass and weeds.

A scruffy blonde in a leather jacket finished off his beer, tossed the can over his shoulder and opened another. He took a swig just as one of his cohorts leaned over to deliver the punch line of a joke. The blonde laughed uproariously, spraying beer all over the headstone next to the fallen one on which his butt was perched. Another partygoer clambered to his feet and wandered off into the shadows only to return a minute later, zipping his fly.

Nick watched the goings-on with disgust. These animals had no respect for sacred ground. Or any other ground, as far as he could tell.

Over the past several weeks, he'd learned that the repulsive crew had ridden down from Baltimore, about twenty miles north, to enjoy the rural atmosphere of Howard County. School playgrounds, local parks, old cow pastures—they'd put their unique stamp on a number of spots. But Ten Oaks Cemetery seemed to be their favorite. Unfortunately for them.

The small burial ground was a stark contrast to Dayton Acres, a new development of two-story colonials that stood only a cornfield away. Not surprisingly, the owners weren't eager to share their costly locale with a bunch of crude invaders. They'd complained to the cops, who had come out a few times but, failing to catch the bikers in any illegal acts, had more or less washed their hands of the problem.

Frustrated but determined, the homeowners' association had taken matters into its own hands and hired Nick.

As Nick watched, two of the big lugs pushed over a gravestone. It fell to the ground with a thud and cracked in half.

"Oops!"

The witticism drew a burst of laughter from the leather-clad crowd.

"Okay, gentlemen, it's time," Nick muttered. He was going to enjoy scaring the spit out of these worthless jerks.

He was wearing one of his favorite outfits, a reproduction of an eighteenth-century highwayman's costume—black shirt, black britches and high black boots. In his machine shop, he'd made two flintlock replicas, except instead of holding a single shot, they each held a sixteen-shot clip filled with blanks. He stuck the weapons into his belt, then donned the other props he'd brought— a hood and vest, both black. The hood was painted like a skull, while the vest was adorned with ribs and vertebrae, all in white fluorescent paint.

He hated to resort to cheap tricks, but he figured it was the fastest, cleanest way to get rid of these brainless slobs. And, really, he couldn't suppress an evil grin as he imagined his quarries' reactions to the surprise he had in store for them.

Halloween costume in place, he drew one of the pistols and stepped from under the shadows of the maple. In the next instant, he charged.

Moving with superhuman speed, feet barely touching the ground, he zoomed toward the gang. At the last second, just before reaching the blonde, he veered off, whipping past the little cemetery like a creature who had clawed his way up from one of the graves.

"Wha' the hell was that?" one of the bikers gasped.

"Dunno," his companion replied.

Nick changed his angle of attack. Weaving among the headstones, using the moves he'd learned in one of the video games he liked to play, he fired off a couple of blanks. Like a wraith out of "Phantom Combat," he reached out with his free hand to knock over a couple of the revelers as he sped past.

The two guys cried out as they hit the ground. The women who'd come for fun and games screamed like banshees. Nick let loose with his best *Tales from the Crypt* cackle, then fired off a couple more shots.

By the time he wheeled around for another pass, the bikers and their lady friends were scrambling for their hogs. Only one of them was dumb enough to stay and challenge the supernatural intruder who had interrupted their party.

Nick recognized the moron as Butch McCard, the unofficial leader of the group. Reaching into his boot, McCard pulled out a small pistol and fired in Nick's general direction. The bullet took a chunk off the top of a headstone five or six feet away.

"Big mistake," Nick growled, zooming toward the shooter like a monster escaped from a horror movie, firing blanks from the pistols as he went.

The guy stumbled backward a few paces. "No! Please! Don't kill me!"

"Be gone!" Nick roared. Suiting action to words, he shoved his pistol into his belt and jammed his hands into McCard's armpits. Lifting the two-hundred-plus-pound man as if he were a bag of lemons, Nick tossed him so hard that he landed twenty feet away, in the cornfield beside the burial ground.

The jerk lay still for a moment, gasping for breath. Then he scrambled up and dashed toward his bike.

The engine wouldn't start, and he desperately cranked the ignition, cursing like a sailor. When his bike roared to life, he didn't even look back as he raced away into the night.

Nick stood at the edge of the cemetery, watching the departing figure and fighting a vague feeling of disappointment. The bikers hadn't been much of a challenge.

Turning, he surveyed the beer cans and fast-food wrappers littering the ground. Cleanup wasn't part of his job, but he returned to his hiding place, shucked his skeleton costume and pulled out the plastic garbage bag he'd brought along. He left the trash neatly at the side of the access road. Then, finished with the night's work, he walked across the field to the car he'd hidden behind a tangle of honeysuckle vines, and headed for home.

He'd purchased the Victorian farmhouse and surrounding twenty-five acres when prices were still reasonable. From the outside, none of the eccentric renovations he'd made showed, changes made to bring the place up to his specifications—along with a few ideas borrowed from Batman.

The garage was underground, the ramp hidden by a door that looked like a wooden retaining wall. Behind the garage were his workshop and laboratory. He'd made certain that the contractor who had done the work would never tell anyone about it.

As far as the interior of the house went, Nick had done most of the work himself, utilizing some of the useful skills he'd acquired over the years. As he walked through the lower level to the restored first floor and looked around, he felt a familiar sense of satisfaction. His home was a showplace decorated with eighteenth- and nineteenth-century antiques. He'd made a satisfying life for himself here, and he intended to hang on to it as long as he could. Which was why he kept to himself. None of his neighbors and only a few of his clients had ever set foot inside the house, and he meant to keep it that way.

And yet...

His gut was telling him that change was coming. It had overtaken him too often in the past for him not to feel the vibrations. He wasn't ready for it—he never was—but if time had taught him anything, it was that change was inevitable. It would come whether or not he was ready and, good or bad, he would have to face it.

Something else he'd learned—worrying about the future was energy wasted.

Moving quickly, he strode down the hall to his office, where his computer appeared as a strangely modern addition to the Winthrop desk on which it sat. Pulling up his chair, he typed a report on the evening's activities for the Dayton Acres Community Association, attached a bill and e-mailed it to the organization's president.

Not that he needed the money. He could have lived very nicely on his investments. But having once "enjoyed" a life of leisure, he knew he'd be bored witless inside a week if he didn't keep busy.

He checked his e-mail for the next chess move from his opponent in Quito, Ecuador. Juan had moved his knight into a position that would prove vulnerable six moves down the line. In the library he moved the piece to its new position.

Work and play finished for the night, he went downstairs to the basement to set the alarm system—not a conventional alarm but something a lot more creative that he'd invented in his spare time. After crossing the unfinished section of the basement, he stepped through a doorway that led into a completely different environment: his private living quarters, with its comfortable lounge and bedroom, and an admittedly sybaritic bathroom.

Sleep tugged at him. Yet he sat for an hour on the wide leather couch in the lounge, surfing the hundreds of television channels beamed in through his satellite dish. He used all six screens, flicking through multiple images in four languages—English, Spanish, French and Arabic.

He knew why he was avoiding the inevitability of sleep, and in the privacy of his own thoughts, he could acknowledge the cowardice involved. He didn't want to face the dreams that had been disturbing his slumber for the past few weeks.

Sometimes they were scenes from long ago, scenes that he had struggled to banish from his mind. He saw Jeanette again. He saw himself, bound and helpless. He saw a monster—a monster he recognized—leading Jeanette off to her death.

Then, as his dreaming self watched in confusion, Jeanette was transformed. Her sophisticated French upsweep had become straight, shoulder-length and blond. Her large brown eyes changed to blue, her small rosebud mouth widened into full, sensual lips and her complexion paled.

He was dreaming about another woman. He was certain he'd never met her, yet she returned again and again to haunt his sleep. At first, the dreams had all been nightmares of her death. Lately, though, things had taken a very different turn.

He'd be holding Jeanette in his arms, kissing her, making sweet love to her with all the tender emotions he had felt so long ago. And then, suddenly, it was the other woman he was holding, and all the passion he'd learned to keep tightly in check was unleashed. Their clothing vanished, and they were skin-to-skin close, chest to breasts, legs tangling together amid silky-soft sheets. His mouth devoured hers as he caressed her breast with one hand and, with the other, searched to find the slick heat between her legs. She lay back on the bed and held out her arms, and he came down on top of her...then awoke, blood pounding, breathing ragged, body covered with sweat.

He squeezed his eyes shut, struggling to banish the heated scene from his mind. He didn't want to dream. Not of the few sweetly tender moments of love he'd shared with Jeanette, nor of her death or the fiend who had caused it. And certainly not of wildly erotic lovemaking with a woman who, if she even existed, he'd never met and could never hope to have.

Finally, when his body dictated that sleep was his only option, Nick wearily undressed and lay down on his bed. His last conscious thought was to hope that the dreams would leave him be.

"DAMIEN WANTS to speak to you." The message was delivered with a verbal smirk that set Emma Birmingham's teeth on edge.

Without glancing over her shoulder, she finished tucking in the sheet at the side of her narrow bed, one of eight in the crowded room where she'd been sleeping for the past couple of weeks. Shoulders tensed, she turned inquiringly toward Henry Briggs, the man who had shattered the relative tranquility of her morning—if anyone could be tranquil after so many nights of the same highly erotic but still unnerving dream she'd been having.

"Don't keep him waiting," Briggs added in a silky voice that carried more than a hint of warning.

Emma kept her own tone calm. "I'll be right there. Just let me comb my hair and put on a little lipstick."

"The Master will like you well enough without the primping."

She started to offer a stinging retort, then clamped her mouth closed. Briggs was one of the men in Caldwell's inner circle, and it was dangerous to anger him.

Quickly, before she could get herself into trouble, she grabbed her brown suede purse from the nightstand and slipped into the adjoining communal bathroom. Thankfully, her roommates had already gone to breakfast, so she had the bathroom to herself.

The face that peered back at her from the mirror was taut with anxiety, and Emma struggled to coax a dreamy look into her blue eyes. She'd seen that look often enough among the women, her sister, Margaret, included, who drifted like Stepford wives around the Refuge.

Her own mind was still functioning independently, but the place was getting to her in insidious ways. Not a night went by now that she wasn't waking from the same shockingly vivid dream. At first, she'd had only nightmares, most of them about her own death—at the hands of Damien Caldwell.

In the past week, though, a new dream had replaced the nightmares. A dream about a darkly handsome man she had never met, yet he knew her, mind, body and soul, as no one else ever had.

Her dream lover came to her out of a misty darkness, taking her into his arms, kissing and caressing her and soothing away all her fears—until he vanished, leaving her hot and frustrated.

She dragged in a breath and let it out slowly and evenly, reminding herself why she was staying in this scary little community.

A month ago she'd gotten a letter from her twin sister burbling about how she'd come to the Refuge for a self-actualization seminar and decided to stay. Emma knew it shouldn't have surprised her. Their own mother had been a dud at raising a family, and Margaret was always searching for a sense of stability, of security, of home. Joanie Patterson had been married four times and had lived with more than a dozen guys. Luckily for her, only one of the marriages had resulted in offspring—twins—so she'd only had two daughters to neglect while she focused on the series of men in her life.

With the uncanny intuitive bond identical twins often shared, Margaret and she had taken turns mothering each other, with Margaret far more likely than Emma to get the laundry done or a hot dinner on the table when Mom failed to show.

The lack of actual parenting had made Emma independent, self-reliant, freewheeling. She'd been in and out of so many brief relationships that Margaret had warned her she'd end up like their mother if she wasn't careful. The warning had brought her up short, and she'd been cautious—and unsatisfied—ever since.

She and her twin might look alike, but their personalities were very different. In fact, their home life had had just the opposite effect on her sister. Margaret was always solicitous and caring, but introverted and a bit insecure. While Emma had pursued her dream of becoming an artist who created beautiful pieces of silver jewelry, her sister had worked summers and afternoons in the quiet of a health food store and, later, as an accountant. And she had never stopped looking—unsuccessfully—for a father figure in the men she dated.

So at first Emma had been delighted to find out that Margaret was attending a self-actualization seminar in Maryland. It sounded as if her twin was branching out, and her latest enthusiasm wasn't simply another inappropriate older man.

Yet something about her sister's letter, saying she was staying indefinitely at the Refuge, had triggered Emma's "twin intuition." She had sensed that not all was well with her sister, so she had looked up Damien Caldwell on the Internet.

What she'd learned about him had made her stomach clench, starting with the title he'd made up for himself—the Master. She wanted to know where he had come from and how he'd become so successful so quickly, but there was no information about him prior to two years ago, when he'd bought the Refuge after the millionaire who owned it had died.

Since then, it appeared that Caldwell had run the estate—really, more like an entire enterprise—as a cult or a commune, using his self-help seminars as a lure to rope in converts. Apparently if the people who attended the seminars were susceptible to his...his what? Charisma? Mind control? then he would invite them to stay on.

Unfortunately, Margaret had turned out to be one of them. No surprise, really, given that the Master exuded "paternal" authority.

Worried about her sister, Emma had signed up for Caldwell's weekend-long seminar. She'd hoped that, face-to-face, Margaret would respond to her, as she always had. But their former connection seemed to be lost, replaced by her twin's devotion to Caldwell.

Worried sick and unable to abandon her sister, Emma had managed to come across as "worshipful" enough to be asked to stay at the Refuge—at least on a trial basis.

But this was the second time in the past few days that the Master had asked to see her alone. Why?

Did he know that in the middle of the day, when everyone was busy, she'd been sneaking around the mansion, looking through his private papers? Lord, if someone had seen her and told Caldwell, she was a dead woman. And she feared that was no exaggeration. People had disappeared from the Refuge. Usually it happened in the middle of the night, when everyone was sleeping. The next day, it was as if the person had never even existed, as far as the zombies living here were concerned.

Knowing she couldn't keep Caldwell waiting any longer, she splashed cold water on her face and dried off with a paper towel. Then she hurried down the hall to the stairs.

The Master's study was at the back of the mansion. As she stood before the closed door, she ordered her heart to stop pounding. It failed to cooperate.

"Come in," his deep voice called out in response to her knock. "And close the door."

As she stepped into the room, her gaze focused immediately on the man's broad shoulders and shaggy dark hair, which he wore at shoulder length. That and his black coat made him look a little like a taller version of Johnny Cash in his prime. But there was nothing folksy about Damien Caldwell. He radiated a malevolent power. At least that was how he came across to her. A lot of other people, including her sister, obviously saw him differently.

He was standing by the French doors, gazing

out across the manicured lawn that sloped down to the Miles River, but he turned from the window, fixing her with his penetrating gaze—more intense than the eyes of any other man she had met. She knew many people—both men and women—had lost themselves in their fathomless depths.

To distract herself, she focused on a tree outside the window.

"Thank you for coming, my dear. I know you must be eager to get to breakfast," he said in the gravelly voice that grated on her nerve endings. His accent was strange—not anything she could identify except to know that it wasn't American.

"I'm always glad to see you," she answered.

"But you're nervous," he countered.

"Yes. Your personality is so…magnetic. When I'm with you, it's hard for me to think."

"Just relax. I wanted to compliment you on your work. How are you getting on with the other silversmiths?" he asked.

"Very well," she answered, hoping it was true, now that she had tamped down her creative flair for design.

Caldwell had a genius for discovering people's talents and putting them to work for the good of the commune. Some Refuge residents traveled to Baltimore every day to work in offices and bring their paychecks "home." Some ran his e-mail-based publications business. Others did publicity for his seminars. Margaret was kept busy doing his bookkeeping. And still other residents, like her, had special talents that Caldwell could exploit.

Emma had learned her craft from Betty Blanchard, a master silversmith in Manitou Springs, Colorado. Two years after starting to work with Betty, she'd begun supporting herself on the sales from her original jewelry, first as an employee, then as a partner. Thank God Betty had been okay with her rushing off to Maryland. She understood the twin thing.

Caldwell moved from his place beside the window, gliding toward her almost as if his feet didn't need to touch the floor. He stopped directly in front of her.

When he reached out a hand, she looked down at it. To her surprise, his nails were yellow and brittle, with grooves running from the nail beds to the tips. Even though his skin was smooth, those nails made him look a hundred years old.

She stood very still while he stroked her shoulder-length hair, her cheek, the side of her neck, her back.

Closing her eyes, she endured his touch. But when his hand drifted to the top of her breast, she took a quick step away.

"Don't," she said softly.

"You don't enjoy intimacy?"

She had heard the women talking about their sexual experiences with Caldwell and had considered what to say if he put the moves on her. "I've had some bad experiences with men. That makes me cautious—even with you."

He tipped his head to one side, studying her. "Speaking your mind is one of the qualities that makes you stand out."

"Thank you," she whispered. "If you meant it as a compliment."

"I'm thinking about how I mean it," he said with a chuckle.

But she wasn't fooled. He truly was weighing her merits, and she was sure her very life hung in the balance.

"You should go on, before you miss breakfast."

"Thank you," she murmured, and she exited the room.

She had to get out of here. But how could she leave Margaret at this place?

She couldn't. Not alone.

It was extremely hard for Emma to admit she needed help. If her mother's example had taught her anything, it was that the only person she could rely on—besides Margaret—was herself. Now Margaret was lost to her. And every day she spent at the Refuge had driven her closer to the conclusion that this was a situation she couldn't handle on her own.

So she had come up with Plan B.

The star of the not-fully-formulated plan was a man named Nicholas Vickers. She didn't know him, but she thought he might help her. During her snooping in Caldwell's office, she'd found a thick folder on Vickers, containing a lot of notes about his job as a private detective, as well as his personal life.

Reading between the lines, she'd gathered that Vickers and Caldwell were mortal enemies. She didn't know why, exactly, but she had the feeling the animosity had something to do with a woman. Maybe someone Vickers had loved had come to the Refuge for a weekend seminar and had been brainwashed into staying. Whatever the case, she knew something bad had happened between the two men in the past. And she knew that Caldwell considered Nicholas Vickers a threat. Coming from the Master, that was a powerful endorsement.

She'd begun thinking of Vickers as a possible ally. As her own sense of helplessness had grown, she'd started pinning her hopes on him, praying he could help her get Margaret out of here. Maybe because she was stuck in such an untenable situation, she'd actually started daydreaming about his charging in here on a white horse and sweeping her and Margaret to safety.

Caldwell hadn't included a picture of the man in his files, but she'd made up a persona for Nicholas Vickers. And she was pretty sure she had started dreaming about him, too. He was totally appealing with his dark good looks, quick mind and muscular body. A dangerous opponent, yet a man with compassion. An expert lover, knowing and strong, able to bring her both intense fulfillment and complete contentment. Not a bad man to have around to help her forget, for a little while, about this horrible place she so desperately needed to escape.

There was a flaw in her scenario, of course. She always awoke from the dreams sweaty, tangled in her sheet and unsatisfied.

And then she'd tell herself sex wasn't the important issue. The important thing was convincing him to help her rescue Margaret. Was that crazy? Pinning her hopes on a man she didn't know? Maybe she was just as wacky as everyone else here. She was sane enough, however, to realize that Nicholas Vickers could never live up to her fantasies about him, either as a lover or a rescuer of deluded women like Margaret. But he was the only hope Emma had, so she'd memorized his name, address and phone number.

A man passed her in the hall, giving her a speculative look, and she realized she was standing like a statue in the corridor.

Ducking her head away from him, she hurried to the communal dining room. Relieved to find it almost empty, she grabbed a piece of toast from the buffet—then hurried out to the workshop.

## Chapter Two

At the end of the day, Damien Caldwell stood at the open French doors, watching the sun set across the river, admiring the glorious pinks and oranges of the sky. The sunset was a gift of nature, as were the green lawns and the flower beds his workers tended so diligently.

Long ago, he had thought he would never see the daylight again. But his skills and endurance had given it back to him, and it had never shone on a more lovely, bucolic setting than the one where he'd founded his latest commune.

There had been many such enclaves over the years—in France, Germany, Corsica, Italy, Turkey. He had lived in many lands. And he had amassed great wealth and power.

He chuckled. For a boy who had been born a slave, he'd done very well for himself. That long-ago boy had dreamed of changing the rules, of being the one to crack the whip and make the life-

and-death decisions. Fate had given him the chance to realize the dream. Of course, his methods weren't exactly politically correct by modern standards. He lived by rules he'd learned centuries ago. His hero was still that shining example of despotism, Machiavelli. And nobody had ever given him a reason to change his philosophy.

He'd come to the United States—the land of opportunity—early in the nineteen hundreds and settled in Pennsylvania. From there, he'd moved to northern California, then to southern Georgia. He always kept his eye out for property that suited his needs. As it happened, he'd heard the Refuge was for sale at a time when Georgia had become...uncomfortable for him. And so he'd become a resident of Maryland's quaint, easy-paced eastern shore.

The fifty-acre estate was very private, yet close enough to both the Baltimore and Washington metro areas that his followers could keep their jobs while they served him.

A deferential tap on the door brought Damien out of his musings. "Come in," he called.

Henry Briggs entered, closing the door behind him. Briggs was one of his most trusted lieutenants—trust being a relative term.

"What about Emma Birmingham?" Damien asked.

"She did her work all right," Briggs replied. "But all day she was jumpy as a bullfrog on a griddle."

"I was afraid of that. She's been pretending to fit in, but she's not really one of the chosen."

"No."

"Doubtless, she's here to try to convince her sister to leave."

Henry made a sound of agreement. He was the perfect yes man.

"I'm going to hold one of my special ceremonies tomorrow night. The lovely Emma Birmingham will be the sacrifice."

"You want me to scoop her up and put her in a holding cell?"

Damien shook his head. "Not yet. Let her make her beautiful jewelry one more day." He waited a beat, then added, "And, Henry, make certain you get the right woman. Emma looks very much like Margaret."

"I know which is which. Emma's the one with the crafty eyes."

"Yes." Damien nodded toward the door. "Leave me, now."

After Briggs left, Damien moved restlessly around the room. He would take Emma Birmingham's life. First, though, he wanted to take her sexually. She would never come willingly to his bed, so he would wait until she was in the holding cell. Then he could do anything he wanted.

EMMA STOOD in the darkness outside Caldwell's office, her heart pounding wildly in her chest. She had to struggle not to sprint away like a frightened cat. If she did, Caldwell was sure to hear her.

When she'd seen where Henry Briggs was going, she'd ducked around the side of the house and crept up to the open French doors, praying that Caldwell wouldn't step outside and catch her.

The conversation she overheard confirmed her worst fears. She hadn't been fooling anybody. Caldwell knew her devotion to him was faked, and he'd made up his mind what to do about it. Unless she got out of here before tomorrow night, she was a dead woman.

She'd never been to one of his special ceremonies. They were attended only by his inner circle of followers. Once, when she was standing on the dock by the river, she had heard an eerie chanting coming from the grove in the woods where everyone knew the ceremonies took place. The sound had raised the hairs on the back of her neck. Something dark and ugly went on at those so-called ceremonies—she was sure of it. Now she knew it for a fact.

And she was slated to be the main attraction for the next one.

She had to get out of here. Now.

But how? How would she get past the guards and the electric fence? The chances were slim, and with Margaret in tow, they plummeted to near zero.

Emma's fingers knitted together until they hurt as she tried to figure out what to do. Fantasies of being rescued by her dream lover, Nicholas Vickers, were just that—fantasies. She had to get herself and Margaret away from here on her own. And while she stood there in the gathering darkness, hidden by the shrubbery, a desperate plan began to form in her mind.

The question of whether it was hopeless to try to convince Margaret to leave had become irrelevant. She'd run out of time. Somehow she'd have to trick Margaret into leaving. The alternative—escaping alone—was…well, she just wouldn't be able to live with herself if she abandoned her sister.

At dinner, Emma slipped away early, pretending she had to go to the bathroom. Then she hurried to her room and grabbed her purse.

Downstairs again, she waited for Margaret to come out of the dining room with the rest of the crowd.

Her sister spotted her immediately. "You were gone a long time."

Forcing a little smile, Emma replied, "Yes, I stepped outside to admire the view."

"It's getting dark."

"And it's a lovely night. Let's go down by the river, Marg."

Margaret looked over her shoulder at the people headed for the common rooms inside the mansion. In the evening, they usually listened to music or played games like checkers and Monopoly, or they went to lectures given by Caldwell.

"Are you sure it's okay to go out?" Margaret asked.

"Perfectly." Emma took her sister's arm. "It's a step toward self-actualization, a merging of your spirit with the cosmos."

The platitude came straight from a Caldwell lecture, and, thank God, Margaret seemed to recognize it. After a little resistance, she allowed herself to be led from the mansion and down the path toward the water.

Emma knew the way quite well. She had explored the grounds as much as possible, while being careful not to attract attention, looking for quick exits. Caldwell had a cabin cruiser moored at the end of the dock, but even if she had the key, the cruiser was beyond her navigational abilities.

The rowboat she'd spotted yesterday, however, was not. She was relieved to see that it was still pulled up on the beach near the pier, small waves lapping gently at its hull.

Emma looked out over the water. The Miles River wasn't all that wide—less than a mile, she guessed, at the point where she stood—and she was in good shape. She could row the small boat to the opposite shore. Once she got Margaret that far…

Well, one step at a time. She'd worry later about how she'd convince her brainwashed sister to keep traveling away from the Refuge.

Of course, they'd be leaving behind everything they'd brought with them, including the car she'd rented at the airport. But that was nothing compared to their lives.

Fighting to keep her tone light and casual, she said, "Remember when we were kids, when Mom was married to Larry?"

"He was a jerk," Margaret huffed.

"Yeah, but a rich jerk."

Margaret chuckled—an encouraging sound given her near-robotic state. If she could still laugh, maybe she was still capable of thinking about something besides the crap Damien Caldwell had drummed into her head.

"Remember Larry had that cottage up at Moonlight Lake?" Emma said. "We'd go swimming there."

After a brief pause, Margaret replied, "That was fun."

"Yeah, it was. And sometimes we'd take his boat out."

"We were too young to be doing that unsupervised," Margaret said in a tone that echoed her old, ultraresponsible persona.

"Well, we're not too young to do it now." Emma gestured toward the rowboat. "Let's go for a ride. You can be captain—just like the old days."

Her sister eyed the small craft. "I don't think we're supposed to go for boat rides. We'd better ask first."

Emma felt her desperation rising. "If you ask and they say no, I'll be really disappointed. Come on." She tugged on her sister's arm. "Let's just do it. Do it for me, Marg."

Margaret dug her heels into the sand and eyed the water. "It's getting dark and...sort of spooky."

"No, it isn't. It's beautiful. Look at the stars. You used to love the night sky, remember? We'd lie on our backs and you'd point out constellations. I've forgotten them, though, so you could show them to me again."

"No!" Suddenly Margaret let out a high-pitched yelp and shoved her away.

"Quiet! Someone will hear you," Emma ordered, reaching for her sister.

But Margaret kept backing away. "I know what you're trying to do, Emma. You're trying to kidnap me. They warned me that you might."

"Shhh!" She tried to cover Margaret's mouth—

and felt her sister's teeth sink into her finger. "Ow! Margaret, stop it! Someone's going to hear us."

"Good! I want them to hear me. I'm going to find the men and tell them what you're doing. You never really embraced Damien's lessons—his wisdom and kindness. I know you, Emma. I know you're too independent to be a follower of *any* philosophy, no matter how good and true it is. You've been lying to me—and, worse, to the Master—saying you believe. But you don't and you never will." Margaret wrenched herself from Emma's grasp and started running.

As she watched her sister's retreating back, Emma felt her throat clog with tears. Now what? Knock her sister out and drag her onto the damned boat?

When she started to follow Margaret, Emma heard her sister shouting, "It's my sister! She's trying to kidnap me! I need help!" And in that instant, Emma saw her choices swept away.

She had to leave. Now.

Before they could catch her, she pushed the little boat into the water. Then she climbed in, sat on the center seat and grabbed the oars, conveniently left ready in the oarlocks. It had been a long time since she'd rowed a boat, but it came back to her. She maneuvered the craft around, pointing the bow at the opposite bank, then began rowing in earnest, the oar tips digging deep into the dark water. As she pulled swiftly away from the shore, she glanced over her shoulder and saw Margaret running down the path—followed by two of the guards.

"Come back!" one of them shouted.

It was fully dark now, but the pole light at the end of the dock provided all the illumination necessary for her to see the man taking off his shoes and slacks. Oh, God, he was coming after her.

In the next instant, a volley of bullets sprayed the water, missing the boat by inches.

Emma cursed, wishing she had a weapon to defend herself. Ted, another of her stepfathers, had been big into self-protection, and he'd dragged them all, her mother included, to the shooting range on a regular basis. At the time she'd hated any suggestions that came from the creep, but she'd since come to appreciate knowing her way around firearms.

Not that the knowledge was doing her a bit of good right now. She'd been afraid to bring a gun with her to the Refuge. Which meant her only option was to row like hell until she was out of range—and hope the gunman's aim didn't improve.

She thought she must have succeeded when the shooting stopped. She breathed out a sigh of relief—then heard a splash that told her the guy who'd been stripping on the dock had plunged into the river.

In quick over-the-shoulder glances, she saw him swimming toward her—and catching up. Groaning, she forced her burning arm muscles to row faster until, finally, she was outpacing him. By the time she was three quarters of the way across the river, he gave up and turned around.

She muttered a prayer of thanks, knowing she wasn't home free. For all she knew, Caldwell had people stationed on the other side of the river. All it would take was a call to a cell phone, and his goons could be waiting to snatch her when she landed. Even if the guards weren't already in place, they could drive over the bridge a few miles upstream and still be there to catch her.

In all of her life, Emma had never been so frightened. With the palms of her hands blistering and her muscles screaming under the strain of pulling the oars, she rowed for her life—and for Margaret's. She had come this far, had escaped Caldwell's horribly misnamed Refuge, and she could damn well make it the rest of the way.

She *had* to make it. For herself and for Margaret.

A speedboat came racing up the river. It seemed to be heading directly toward her, and her whole body went rigid. What if it was full of Caldwell's men? Or what if it rammed into her in the darkness? Either way, she'd be dead. As the speedboat came closer, she prepared to leap over the side of the rowboat.

When the larger craft sped by, she sagged in relief. She could hear people laughing and talking—vacationers, probably, or local residents out having fun on the river. For a minute or two, she slumped over the oars, breathing hard.

She wanted to curse at her sister for turning her in—for getting them both into this mess in the first place. But she knew it wasn't Margaret's fault. Her mind was like a sponge for Caldwell's orders, and she was behaving as he had trained her to act. How long did Margaret have before her brain turned completely to mush? Was there a point beyond which she would be irrevocably lost?

Or would something even worse happen? Would Caldwell punish Margaret for her sister's disobedience?

Emma straightened, her gaze fixed on the moonlit shoreline ahead. In her effort to save Margaret, had she, in fact, signed her twin's death warrant?

Should she go back?

The rowboat had lost its forward momentum and was drifting with the current. She let it drift, while she sat caught in a storm of emotions more intense and painful than anything she'd experienced in a very long time.

She might have gone on sitting there, trapped by indecision, if a single thought hadn't finally bubbled to the surface of the turmoil inside her head: Nicholas Vickers.

He would know what to do. He could help her save Margaret. She just had to find him and…and what? Tell him to don his armor, saddle his white charger and come to her rescue?

Emma snorted in self-disgust. How stupid could she be, pinning all her hopes on a stranger? She had no control over her subconscious, the irrational part of her that had turned Vickers into her ideal man—Sir Galahad and the perfect lover rolled into one. But common sense and experience told her that he would turn out to be just a regular, ordinary guy, nothing special. If she was lucky—and it was a big "if"—he wouldn't be a complete jerk. And he would help her.

She needed help. That much was crystal clear. Desire and determination weren't enough. She lacked the skills and training necessary to free Margaret, willing or not, from Caldwell and his guards. If Nicholas Vickers wouldn't lend his expertise to her cause, she'd have to find someone else who would.

Meanwhile, she could only pray that Margaret had bought herself some favorable treatment by trying to abort her sister's escape attempt and by refusing to go with her.

Feeling marginally better for having come to a decision, Emma took note of the rowboat's position. The shore was only a couple of hundred yards away—a good thing, since her arms and shoulders felt like rubber. It occurred to her, though, that enough time had passed that Caldwell's goons could well be waiting to pick her up when she landed.

She allowed the boat to drift past several docks belonging to large estates. Finally, when she thought she'd gone far enough downstream, she gathered what was left of her strength, rowed the rest of the way to shore and climbed out.

She started to pull the boat onto the beach, then hesitated, realizing she might as well post a sign that read This is Where Emma Birmingham Landed. She should probably sink the boat. Or she could use it as a decoy.

Giving the boat a shove, she pushed it into the water again, wading in to give it another good shove, then watching as the current grabbed it and took it away. With a little luck, it would serve to throw the Refuge guards off her trail. They might even think she'd drowned.

Exhausted and bedraggled, she looked around to get her bearings.

In front of her was a scraggly wood, full of underbrush, but a little way to the right lay a wide expanse of well-tended lawn. And on that lawn, set well back from the river, was a very large house with lights showing in many of its windows. Maybe the people inside would help her.

Or shoot her as an intruder. Or set the family Rottweilers on her. That, she thought, would really be the final straw.

Yet if she walked to the road, Caldwell's men could be waiting to scoop her up.

She swiped a hand through her hair and sighed. Given the choices, she decided, the house was the lesser of the evils. She started toward it, but she hadn't trudged more than twenty feet when a large, masculine hand clamped down on her shoulder.

She opened her mouth to scream—but she didn't have the chance. The man's other hand clamped itself firmly over her mouth.

# Chapter Three

Emma twisted in her captor's arms. Shooting out a foot, she caught him in the shin and was gratified to hear him grunt. But he didn't let her go. She managed another kick, and he muttered a curse.

"Take it easy," he said. "I'm not going to hurt you."

*Like hell.* She kept struggling and pounding him with all her strength, determined to go down fighting.

"If you've escaped from Caldwell's estate, I'm on your side," he puffed. "So stop trying to do me bodily harm."

When she kept fighting, his voice took on an urgent note. "I'll trust you, if you trust me. I'll take my hand off your mouth if you promise not to scream. Nod if you agree."

She could always change her mind later.

She nodded, and when he took his hand away,

she spun around to face him. "Who are you?" she demanded.

"Alex Shane. With the Light Street Detective Agency. I was hired to investigate the disappearance of a woman named Anabel Lewis. I have reason to think she's at the Refuge. Do you know her?"

Feeling light-headed, as if she might actually faint, Emma tried to gather her wits. "Anabel. Yes. I do know her. She sleeps in the room next to mine."

"So she's okay?"

"As okay as you can be at the Refuge."

"Tell me about it." He looked around. "Let's get out of here."

"How did you find me?"

"I was doing some surveillance, and I saw you on Caldwell's dock—fighting with some woman. Then I heard shouting, and I saw you take off in the rowboat."

Emma sighed. "The woman is my sister. She ratted me out to Caldwell's guards. She's… This isn't going to make any sense to you, I know, but she's under some kind of mind control—brainwashed, or something. That's what Caldwell does to people. Your Anabel Lewis is in the same shape."

"It does make sense. But come on, we'd better get out of here." As he spoke, he ushered her along the shore.

Suddenly, from the darkness of the woods, she

heard the crackle and tromping of feet running through the underbrush. Then came men's voices, low and urgent.

"This way. I saw her land a few minutes ago."

"But the boat's—"

"I don't give a damn about the boat. I tell you, I saw her land. She's got to be around here somewhere."

Swift as a hawk in the night, Alex Shane grabbed Emma and pulled her into the woods, behind a clump of tall, straight pine trees. A few seconds later, two men rushed past.

She heard the rustle of fabric. Then moonlight glinted off a gun in Shane's hand. Neither one of them spoke as more men moved toward them, their voices lower now.

She felt Shane tense. Lord, would he really shoot these guys? Her knees weakened as the men moved past them.

Shane waited to make sure nobody else was coming, then he took her hand, whispering, "Come on."

Without any urging, she followed as he led her through the woods to the lawn surrounding the well-lit mansion. They skirted the house, then walked through another stand of trees to the edge of the road, where an SUV was parked beneath a tangle of vines. In the darkness, the sweet smell of honeysuckle drifted toward her.

She collapsed into the front seat as Shane started the engine, pulled onto the road and drove away. He didn't turn on his lights, though, until they'd traveled at least a couple of miles.

"So how did you end up at the Refuge?" he asked.

Emma drew a couple of steadying breaths before answering. "My sister took a self-actualization course from Damien Caldwell and decided to burrow in. I came to try to dig her out. That was two weeks ago. I've been pretending to be a believer, but…well, I'm not much of an actress. Caldwell knew I was faking it, and…and I heard him tell one of his henchmen he was going to kill me."

He whistled through his teeth. "Lucky you got away."

"They probably would have snagged me over here if you hadn't come along. Thanks."

"You're welcome. The Refuge is a scary place these days. I've been over by boat, at night, a couple of times." He looked regretful. "If this were the bad old days, I would have stayed and tried to forcibly collect Ms. Lewis. But I've got a wife and two kids now, so risking life and limb is no longer part of the job description."

"You risked your neck just spying over there."

He snorted. "Those odds were acceptable. I worked for the previous owner of the estate,"

Shane continued. "I know what the layout used to be. Tell me what you think has been changed since Caldwell took over—things that look new or like they might have been altered."

"It probably looks likc it always did, except that the bedrooms on the upper floors have been divided up and turned into dormitories, with communal bathrooms added."

"So what are you going to do about your sister?"

She hesitated a moment, questioning the wisdom of sharing her plans with a stranger. But then, the stranger had saved her butt. Besides, she knew intuitively that Alex Shane was on the side of the angels.

"As a matter of fact," she said, "I had another detective in mind."

"Who?" he inquired.

"A man named Nicholas Vickers."

"Don't know him."

Well, so much for recommendations. "Apparently he had a run-in with Caldwell. I'm hoping that puts him on my side."

Shane was quiet for a minute or two. Then, seeming to come to a decision, he said, "If I know an operation is going down, I might be able to get some guys from our agency to act as backup." He reached into his pocket and handed her a card. "As I said, I'm with the Light Street Detective

Agency. The main office is in Baltimore, but I hold down the fort on the eastern shore."

"Thanks," Emma said, taking the card and shoving it into her handbag. They had reached the center of St. Stephens.

"Do you live around here?" Shane asked.

"No, I'm from Manitou Springs, Colorado."

"You're a long way from home." He was silent for a moment, chewing his bottom lip. "It'd be easier for you to evade Caldwell in a city—some place big enough to get lost and stay lost. What if I drive you into Baltimore?"

Again, she had to fight off the tears clogging her throat. "You'd do that for me?"

"Sure." He tossed her a crooked grin. "I admire your grit. Besides, you could turn out to be a valuable witness against Caldwell."

She sighed. "Yeah, but he's careful. And his worshippers are loyal. Even if the cops raided the place tonight, I bet they wouldn't come up with any evidence that would lead to an arrest."

"Caldwell may be careful, but nobody's perfect," Shane said. "He'll have slipped up somewhere. Until we find his Achilles heel, we need to keep you safe. So let me tell my wife I'm driving you across the Bay Bridge."

He pulled the SUV onto the shoulder and picked up his cell phone. Emma listened to his conversation with his wife—she could hardly have avoided it—and was impressed with how warm and close their relationship obviously was.

Funny how it still surprised her that there were people who could make marriage work. She found it reassuring, even if she herself hadn't yet managed the feat. She'd long since stopped getting involved with complete jerks and losers, but it occurred to her that she'd gone to the opposite extreme by dating men so dull and lacking in passion that they bored her to tears.

Maybe, someday, she'd find a middle ground....

"All set." Shane dropped his cell phone into a cup holder, pulled back onto the road and headed out of town.

Exhausted, Emma slumped in her seat and, without meaning to, fell asleep. When she woke, Shane had pulled up in front of a Days Inn.

"You're about three blocks from the inner harbor," he said. "There are lots of places there to shop, if you need to replace your clothes and stuff."

"Thanks, yes, I will have to," Emma replied.

"This hotel isn't the most expensive around, but it isn't cheap." He cleared his throat. "Do you have enough money for the bill?"

"I have a credit card."

He shook his head. "Don't use it. Caldwell could track you if you do."

She checked her wallet. "I've got two hundred in cash."

"That ought to do it."

She turned in her seat to look at him directly. "I don't know how to thank you. I'd never have—"

Shane shook his head. "We're square. You helped me out by sharing your information about the Refuge."

They weren't square. He'd saved her life. "I'm truly grateful."

Emma watched him drive away, then staggered into the hotel lobby.

She wondered if they were going to let her in looking like a refugee from a third-world country.


THE ROUGH-LOOKING MAN had been sitting in the corner of the biker bar for the past hour, nursing a beer and trying not to breathe too deeply. The place smelled like a men's room, with an overlay of booze and cigarette smoke.

Not his kind of scene. But in his two days' growth of beard, uncombed hair and leather jacket, he figured he blended in okay—except for his lack of tattoos and piercings.

A biker with a picture of a cobra decorating his arm swaggered by and propped himself against the bar, allowing room for his beer belly.

"Hey, Snake," one of his buddies called out.

"Yo," the cobra guy answered.

*That's what I need,* the observer thought. *A colorful name. A handle.* He could call himself…Trailblazer. Yeah, Trailblazer would do just fine.

Scanning the crowd at the bar, he shook his head in disgust. It wasn't yet noon, but the place was already full of guys who drank their breakfast. Finally, when he'd had enough of the toxic gas that passed for air, he decided it was time to make his move.

Bellying up to the bar, he ordered another beer. When it came, he took a sip, then turned to the man next to him—a young punk named Butch McCard, the leader of the biker gang and a regular patron of the bar.

"I hear you ran into a little trouble last night," he said to McCard.

McCard's eyes sharpened on him momentarily. "What're you talkin' about?"

"Trouble in Ten Oaks Cemetery," Trailblazer clarified.

McCard's head snapped around. "Keep your nose out of that."

"What if I can help you?"

"How?"

"How about the name of the bastard who broke up your private party?"

Trailblazer kept his face impassive when

McCard grabbed his shirt and demanded, "What the hell do you know about it?"

Trailblazer cautiously shrugged off the offending hand. "We've been keeping an eye on Nicholas Vickers."

"Who is he?"

Jeez, McCard really was a moron. Patiently, he explained, "He's the guy who crashed your party."

"Oh yeah?"

"He sleeps during the day. He sleeps real sound, so you should be able to fix him good without him ever knowing." Seeing the look of interest in McCard's eyes, Trailblazer held out a slip of paper. "You want his address?"

A hammy hand snatched the paper from him. It was almost comical watching the bleary-eyed McCard try to read the address.

"Hey, dude, thanks," the biker said. "What's your name?"

"Trailblazer."

"You want to come with us, Blaze?"

"Naw. Just get him for me."

As McCard strode over to one of his buddies, Trailblazer slipped from the bar and into the morning sunshine, whistling.

NICK STIRRED in his sleep. He was dreaming about a time long ago, when the wife of the Duke of Monmouth had given the cut direct to the wife of the Baron of Bridgewater. The little drama had been the talk of the *ton* for half the social season. He had shaken his head at the gossip, at a society that had nothing more important to focus on than who was snubbing whom.

Suddenly, in the way of dreams, he was somewhere else. It was 1850, and he had taken up residence at a castle outside St.-Paul-de-Vence. He had traveled all through Europe, trying to escape the boredom of his life, looking for some purpose and meaning. Finally, he thought he'd found it— a man who called himself the Master and who promised his followers untold wisdom. He was captivated by the Master's charisma and his idealism so he joined his enclave.

One night, peasants from the region attacked the castle. Without wondering why they would do such a thing, Nick joined in the defense—and got shot in the stomach.

The pain was excruciating, and he knew the wound meant certain death.

"Kill me now. Put an end to it," he begged the Master.

"I may be able to save you," his mentor replied.

"How?"

"How is not important. What matters is, if you survive the process, you will no longer be human. You will be like me. You will live forever. I believe it to be an excellent trade-off, but you must make the decision for yourself."

Barely coherent, in agony from the pain in his gut, his reply came in gasped bursts. "Yes. Do it, please."

The Master sat on the side of the bed and bent toward him, and he felt the first shiver of fear. He had no idea what was about to happen, only a vague sense that, afterward, nothing would ever be the same again. Yet any protest he might have uttered stayed locked in his throat. He did not want to die.

He cried out as he felt the Master's sharp teeth fasten on his neck. And he cried out again as he felt the blood being drawn out of him. Terror shuddered through him but was quickly dispelled by an overwhelming sense of peace and well-being that seemed to invade his mind. The feeling was accompanied by the Master's voice, though he heard no one speaking aloud.

*"Rest,"* the voice said to him. *"You will be well soon. Just rest…."*

Again, Nick tossed in his sleep, shaking his head against the pillow and muttering, "No… don't… God, no…"

As if he had been granted temporary mercy, the scene changed. And suddenly he was in another place, another time.

A pine forest, deep and dark and shrouded in

mist. Through the mist, a woman walked toward him, holding out her arms. A wind blew through the trees, and her hair and her white gown billowed out behind her. *Jeanette,* he thought at first. Then he saw the blond hair and knew it was not she but another woman. The woman whose name he didn't know but who had been haunting his sleep for so many nights.

"Who are you?" he asked her.

She smiled. "We'll meet soon."

"No," he said. "Leave me while you can."

"Let me be with you."

"No!" He gave a near-violent shake of his head. "You don't know what you're asking for."

For a charged moment, neither of them moved. Then, before he could back away, she closed the distance between them and wrapped him in her embrace. Her female scent enveloped him, and the contact of her body pressed to his set up an unbearable ache inside him. When she raised her lips to his, he was lost.

The first touch of his mouth on hers set off sparks that should have set the pine forest ablaze. Heat crackled through him, heat and longing such as he hadn't felt in decades, almost unbearable in its intensity. He knew it was the same for her because she made a small, shocked sound deep in her throat.

That sound was his undoing. That and the soft

caress of her lips against his. They were so sweet and yielding, and at the same time so charged with wild, unvarnished need. Her need kindled his own. He forgot the rules he'd set to govern his life. Forgot about morality and honor. His only reality was the yielding woman he held in his arms.

Gathering her closer, he moved his lips over hers, then sighed in relief as she opened for him. Her mouth was the sweetest thing he had ever tasted. And as he pressed her breasts against his chest, he felt the frantic beating of her heart. Or maybe it was his own heartbeat that he felt. He could no longer tell.

Some rational part of his mind was still issuing warnings. This must stop. He must break away from her before it was too late. But his mouth continued to devour hers, and instead of letting her go, he shifted her in his arms so that he could cup one soft breast. His fingers stroked the hardened tip, wringing a sob of pleasure from her. She pressed against him, silently demanding more, and he gladly gave it.

Picking her up in his arms, he carried her to a table that had materialized out of the mist. He lay her upon it, then began unbuttoning the front of her gown, his shaking fingers clumsy as he undid each button.

Pushing the fabric aside, he looked at her breasts. They were lovely and rounded, the nipples a soft pink and beautifully puckered for him. He slid his fingers back and forth across those tight buds, feeling his whole body go rigid.

He wanted to plunge deep inside her again and again until he found release. And he wanted more—the ultimate joining for the creature he had become. The slits at the sides of his mouth ached with an intensity he had rarely felt. Even when his fangs slid out, the pain didn't go away.

He wanted her blood with a shattering urgency. He felt he would go mad if he didn't taste that part of her.

Tipping her head back, he stroked his tongue against the slender column of her throat. Then he pressed his fangs against her pale skin.

"I want you inside me," she said. "And I want the rest of it, too."

He raised his head and stared down at her. "How do you know about the rest of it?"

She only smiled at him.

Her willingness seemed to bring him partially to his senses. "No, I can't…"

"Do it," she whispered.

"No."

"Are you afraid?" she challenged.

He didn't know the answer. And while he hesitated, the woman evaporated, leaving his arms empty—and his body hot and heavy with unfulfilled need.

Nick clawed his way out of sleep and lay panting on the bed. *Bloody hell.* It had all been so vivid...so *real.* Was the woman a fantasy—something his mind had conjured because he'd been so long abstinent?

Or was she real? And if she was...where was she?

EMMA WOKE disoriented. She had been in the arms of her fantasy lover, Nicholas Vickers. And then he had vanished into thin air. His face was so clear in her mind. Dark, brooding, his eyes deep set, his nose a Roman blade, his jaw square and firm. And his mouth...

Dear Lord, his mouth... It was positively wicked—those deliciously sensual lips tantalizing her skin, that expert tongue exploring her mouth and drawing trails down her neck and across her breasts, and those fine, white teeth, nipping and gently biting and...and something else. Something more about his teeth. Something she didn't want to think about.

She reached out with one hand, sliding it over the cool sheet beside her. She was alone.

Well, of course she was. The man had appeared in her dreams only because she had been focused on him when she went to sleep.

She stretched, still slightly disoriented. The mattress beneath her was soft, the sheets crisp.

They gave off a clean, fresh smell as she moved, rustling them. The blackout blinds at the windows kept all but a slim shaft of light around the edges from filtering through the window.

Without lifting her head from the pillow, she turned to the right and focused on the lighted face of the clock on the bedside table. Ten-thirty! She'd thought she would toss and turn all night and get up early, but she'd slept for a good ten hours.

She had work to do. Every moment she left her sister at the Refuge was a moment too long. She'd debated briefly with herself last night about calling the cops, but she'd quickly decided against it. Margaret hadn't been kidnapped. If she were questioned, she'd say she was at the Refuge of her own free will, as would anyone else the police might ask.

Emma took a hot shower, then got dressed, glad that she'd washed her underwear the night before. It was still a little damp, so she used the hair dryer on it. Dressed in last night's clothes, she took the elevator down to see what she could do about supplementing her wardrobe in the gift shop.

She had just purchased a Charm City T-shirt and was about to step into the lobby when she saw a man approach the front desk. Her blood ran cold when she realized who he was—Mort Frazier, one of the guys from Damien Caldwell's inner circle.

As she stood behind a display rack of scarves near the shop entrance, she watched Frazier approach the desk, which was only a short distance away.

"Can you give me Ms. Birmingham's room number?" he asked the desk clerk politely.

The clerk pulled an apologetic look. "I'm sorry, sir. I'm not allowed to give out that information. You can call her on the house phone."

Frazier grimaced. "I know you're following the rules, but I'm her brother. I don't want to call ahead. She doesn't know I'm in town, and I was hoping to surprise her."

The clerk hesitated.

"Please. She'll love opening her door and seeing me."

Emma waited with her heart pounding.

The clerk looked over her shoulder to make sure nobody on the staff was watching her, then she leaned forward and whispered the room number.

So much for privacy rules. Emma clenched her fists, wishing she had the time to get the woman fired. But then, as Frazier strode to the elevator, she realized that the clerk might have done her a favor. Without her room number, Frazier probably would have waited in the lobby for her to appear. This way, she had a chance to escape before he figured out that she wasn't in her room.

As soon as the elevator doors closed behind him, Emma slipped out the hotel's front entrance and walked rapidly in the direction Alex Shane had said led toward the inner harbor.

She had followed Shane's advice and not used her credit card when she'd booked the room the previous night, but it hadn't occurred to her to use a false name. Had Caldwell's men called a bunch of hotels looking for her? Or did they have some other, secret source of information?

No matter how they'd found her, she'd made a lucky escape. Still, she kept looking over her shoulder as she walked to Light Street, where she found the harbor, restaurants and all kinds of attractions for tourists. At an ATM in a shopping pavilion, she withdrew the daily maximum allowable amount from her account, then she made for the exit. Thinking hard, planning her next move, she crossed the street to the Ramada Renaissance hotel, where she booked a shuttle to BWI Airport, alternating between the lobby and the ladies' room until it arrived.

At the airport, she went to the first rental car company she came to and used her credit card to pay for a vehicle. She had no choice; car rental companies required the use of a credit card, and she required the use of a car. Still, her nerves were jumping until she was on the road again.

She watched the rearview mirror as much as the road ahead until she was well away from BWI.

At a drugstore in a little town called Elkridge, she consulted a phone book, then called the closest gun shop and found out that, in Maryland, since she wasn't under twenty-one or suffering from a mental disorder, she could walk in and buy a gun without a waiting period. An hour later, she had a Sig Sauer P210 tucked into the compartment of her driver's door. Again she used her credit card. Then she cleared out of the area, heading south, toward D.C.

The risk was worth it. With the weapon beside her, she felt a lot more secure.

Her next stop was at a Wal-Mart. She didn't want to show up at Nicholas Vickers's house to ask for help with her clothes looking as if they'd been run through a boot camp obstacle course. She bought clean jeans, a couple of T-shirts, tennis shoes, and a toothbrush and toothpaste. After changing in the ladies' room and brushing her teeth, she felt more like herself. And much more secure about making a decent impression.

Storm clouds were gathering in the west as she consulted the detailed street map she'd picked up in Wal-Mart. With Vickers's address still imprinted on her brain, she quickly saw that she'd been closer to his place in Elkridge. She plotted a circuitous route that would take her northwest, and headed for the private detective's home.

It was a long drive, over an hour, and as the sky grew darker and more ominous, so did Emma's thoughts. An odd sense of fate seemed to be drawing her forward, toward Nicholas Vickers. As if she were seeking him out not merely because he was a private investigator and Damien Caldwell loathed him, but because of her dreams and fantasies as well. As if she and Vickers really did have some intuitive connection, the way she and Marg did—or used to before Damien Caldwell sucked all the autonomy out of Margaret's brain.

All day she'd been focused on getting away from Caldwell's goons and getting to Nicholas Vickers. As her thoughts turned to her twin, she held back tears. Gritting her teeth, she blinked to clear her vision.

She had no time for tears. She had to help her sister. And finding Nicholas Vickers was her best option. She hoped.

When she finally turned onto the rural road where Vickers lived, the clouds hanging low in the sky had turned the afternoon as dark as midnight. Lightning crackled, making her feel as if she were an actor in a horror movie.

The map showed no other access to the narrow, poorly maintained country lane, and no houses peeked through the trees as she drove by. It appeared that Vickers had no close neighbors. Yet when she had gone a few hundred yards, Emma saw a bunch of motorcycles parked on the gravel shoulder beside the crumbling blacktop. Was Mr. Vickers hosting a biker convention?

She slowed the car, craning her neck, looking for the riders, but she saw no one.

The wind began to blow, and a shaft of lightning split the sky, followed a few seconds later by a long roll of thunder. It was followed almost immediately by another flash and, within a shorter interval, another rumble. The storm was going to break soon. Emma sped up, trying to beat the rain.

A little farther along the lane, she rounded a curve and saw a beautiful, large Victorian farmhouse, complete with gingerbread and a wraparound porch. She felt a flood of relief at the sight. It looked so very nice and *normal*.

Her relief was short-lived, dying as soon as she spotted a cluster of tough-looking young men on the left side of the house. Clad in dirty jeans and leather jackets, they were sneaking along, hugging the foundation. One of them was carrying something red. Something that looked suspiciously like a can of gasoline.

NICK WOKE WITH A START. He glanced at the clock and saw that it was just after seven—still well before sunset at this time of year. Unless some-thing unusual happened, he normally slept until dark.

Wondering what was going on outside his private lair, he sat up and reached for the controls that activated the security cameras, which were set to show exterior views of the house. Pressing the remote, he opened the floor-to-ceiling drapes along the wall opposite his bed, uncovering the eight screens that displayed what the cameras were picking up.

Seven of the screens showed nothing out of the ordinary except that the sky was already as black as night. But the eighth riveted his atten-tion.

There, on the east side of his house, he saw the Ten Oaks graveyard gang.

Bloody hell! How the devil had they found him?

As he watched the screen, Nick saw lightning fork through the storm-gathered clouds. A second or two later, he heard a massive clap of thunder. And in the next second, a car pulled into view.

Now what?

Hitting the remote again, he switched on the sound and heard the bikers speaking.

"Hurry up. If it starts to rain, the fire will go out."

"Not with gasoline, man. This old place will go

up like an oil refinery." He punctuated the comment with an evil laugh.

Nick muttered another curse as he leaped out of bed and reached for the black highwayman's britches he'd draped over a chair the night before. Pulling them on and jamming his feet into the high boots, he paused only long enough to turn off the basement alarm system. Then, throwing open the bolt on the door into the storage area, he raced for the stairs.

WIDE-EYED, Emma stared at the man with the gas can as he took off the cap and doused the foundation of Nicholas Vickers's clapboard house. When he pulled a cigarette lighter from his pocket, she grabbed her new gun and jumped out of the car.

"Hold it right there!" she shouted, pointing the automatic at the would-be arsonists.

The guys' heads all jerked up, and to a man, their jaws dropped open in shock.

"Jeez! What's a broad doing here?"

Emma felt her adrenaline pumping, but she managed to keep her voice steady as she replied, "Making sure you don't do something stupid."

"You're the one acting stupid, honey, stickin' your pretty little nose in where it doesn't belong," one of them called out tauntingly, taking a step toward her. "Put the gun down, and we won't hurt you."

In answer, she squeezed off a shot, aiming for the ground right in front of the thug's feet. The bullet kicked up dirt, and the guy stopped in his tracks.

"If you don't want me to aim for your crotch, get the hell out of here."

Some of the gang looked ready to run. But she soon learned that a couple of them had come armed with more than a cigarette lighter. One pulled a small pistol from his boot and raised the weapon. Another pulled an automatic from the waistband of his pants.

Faced with the decision to shoot one of these guys, Emma hesitated a split second too long.

The bikers had no such compunctions. A bullet slammed into her body, and she staggered backward, dropping her gun to wrap her arm around her middle.

"That'll teach you to mess with us," the shooter called out, advancing on her.

He was going to kill her—Emma knew it as surely as she knew her name. Gritting her teeth, she tried to stagger away.

"Where do you think you're going?" he taunted. "You think I can't follow you into the bushes? Come to think of it, that would be kind of fun."

She didn't bother to answer. Then she saw something strange behind the biker.

## Chapter Four

*Bloody hell!* What was she doing here?

No mistaking who she was—he recognized her immediately. The woman from his dreams.

But this was no dream. He was wide awake, and from his vantage point on the porch, Nick saw one of the bikers advancing on the woman, gun in hand, ready to finish the job he'd started. The rest of the low-life animals were watching with wicked grins on their ugly faces.

Roaring like a lion, Nick leaped from the porch and zoomed toward the gunman so fast that he was only a blur in the darkness. Lightning flashed, providing perfect horror-movie effects as he swooped down on the guy. Knocking the weapon from his hand, Nick took him down, slamming him to the ground. For good measure, he stomped on the man's grimy fingers with his boot heel, wringing a scream of pain from him.

He heard the woman gasp, and he looked over

to see her staring at him with a mixture of shock and bewilderment. She was sitting propped against a tree, and he could see she'd been shot in the side. Quickly, he gave her a closer inspection. Seeing no arterial blood gushing, he figured her life wasn't in immediate danger.

Which left him free to terrorize the rest of the criminals who had come to burn him out of house and home.

Wheeling, Nick flew at the gang, scattering them like ants. As they fled, screaming, he went after them one by one. He threw them to the ground, trampled over them with his boots, kicked them in the ribs and back and gut, and ground their faces into the dirt and gravel.

He could easily have killed them. He ached to squash the guy with the gas can. But he kept a tight leash on his anger and settled for scaring the piss out of the burn master, watching the dark stain that spread across the front of the guy's jeans.

Ordinarily, Nick would have pursued the fleeing bikers and wiped the knowledge of the fight—and of the whereabouts of his home—out of their tiny minds. But he had more urgent business. For now, he was confident that they wouldn't be back anytime soon. He could clean up the details later.

When he heard the roar of their motorcycles retreating down his road, he turned to the woman and hunkered down beside her.

She was small and delicate and very beautiful, with blue eyes and shoulder-length blond hair framing her face. Exactly as she'd been in his dreams, to the smallest detail.

Her gaze focused on him, still full of astonishment and confusion. "It *was* you," she whispered. "In my dreams. But how...?"

It was his turn to stare in shock. How, indeed? How had they connected in such an intimate way without ever having met? He knew enough about his powers, and the potential he might someday reach if he worked at it, to know it wasn't out of the realm of possibility that he could bond mentally as he had with her—but not without his conscious decision to do so. And certainly not without knowing if she was even real.

But she *was* real. And she was here, on his doorstep, having arrived at the same time the Ten Oaks gang was in the act of torching his house.

Coincidence? He'd stopped believing in coincidence a long time ago.

Her pained grimace reminded him that, regardless of how she'd gotten here, she was wounded because she'd tried to prevent McCard and his buddies from carrying out their plan.

She glanced over his shoulder, in the direction

the bikers had gone. "How did you do that? How could you be in five places at once?"

"Superhero powers," he answered lightly, knowing she wouldn't take him seriously.

She winced. "My side hurts."

"I'm sorry." He sent her thoughts to ease the pain, feeling her anxiety fade as he worked his magic on her.

Despite the circumstances, the feminine scent of her body drew him to her, as it had in the dreams. But now there was another powerful aroma about her, too—the coppery scent of her blood.

He wanted to taste it. Drink it. He felt the fang slits at the sides of his mouth begin to throb, and he clenched both his fists and his teeth to keep from doing something he would regret.

"Why did you come here?"

She looked up at him with glazed eyes, and he knew she was in shock. "I..."

Instead of finishing the sentence, she raised a hand and touched his bare chest. "The dream was nice, but...this is real," she whispered, combing her fingers through the hair on his chest, her touch raising a shiver that raced across his skin.

The next instant, though, what he felt were raindrops. He'd completely forgotten about the oncoming storm.

"Come on. We have to get you inside," he said,

scooping her up effortlessly in his arms, being careful not to hurt her.

Closing her eyes, she nestled against his bare chest. "Nice," she whispered again.

Ordering himself not to react to her touch or her scent, he hurried to the front porch, then stepped through the open door, kicking it closed behind him.

Her heartbeat seemed to shudder through his own body, and he felt his mind tuning itself to hers. He should put her down, break the contact, yank himself out from under her spell.

That thought confounded him. *He* was the one who wove spells, the one who bent mortals to his will.

Disconcerted and more than a little worried, Nick stood in the hallway, debating where to take her. The rooms upstairs were furnished like bedrooms because he had enjoyed collecting the antiques and using them to create what amounted to stage sets. But they were bound to be dusty. He kept the ground floor in better shape, since he sometimes met with clients here. But there were no bedrooms on this level of the house.

Still undecided, he carried her into the living room and laid her on the Victorian sofa, then perched on the edge of it, beside her. Her eyes were closed, but when he said, "We should get you to the hospital," they flew open.

"No!" she insisted, panic coloring her tone.

"You're hurt. You need medical attention."

"If you take me to the hospital...he'll find me! He already sent a man to my hotel." She tried to drag in a deep breath, then winced at the pain.

"Just lie still," he said.

"You have to listen to me," she begged, clutching at his hand. "Please. I barely...got away."

"From whom?"

"Damien Caldwell."

"Bloody hell!" Nick shot off the sofa, heart pounding as he glared down at her. "Did he send you here?"

"Huh? No." He could see her fighting to speak. "My sister is...one of his...zombies," she managed.

A good way to put it, he thought.

"I went to the Refuge...to get Margaret away from him. Then I heard him...talking to...one of his men. He was...going to kill me." Her face contorted, and she paused again before going on. "Margaret wouldn't leave, and when I tried to get her into a boat..."

Her voice trailed off. Then her eyes fluttered closed, and she lay very still.

"What's your name?" Nick demanded.

A long pause. Then, in a barely audible voice she replied, "Emma Birmingham."

"This is a trick," he said flatly. "Caldwell sent you to...to what? Seduce me into trusting you?"

Her eyes blinked open again, and she focused on him, her brow furrowed. "In the dreams, you were always nice…very nice…."

"Yeah, well, that was just a dream, wasn't it?" he muttered, knowing it wasn't true. Something had already happened between them. Something he didn't understand.

But Caldwell might very well understand it. Nick felt a wave of cold wash through him as he stared down at the woman lying on his couch. He had known Caldwell was getting stronger. Had that demon projected a vision of Emma Birmingham into his mind? Had Caldwell gained so much power that he could do such a thing—and do it without even being in proximity to his victim?

Emma—if that really was her name—tried to push herself to a sitting position but failed. As she fell back against the sofa, her features twisted in pain. Still, she forced her gaze to focus on his, and he knew she was trying to project her sincerity.

"Caldwell didn't send me," she insisted. "You have to believe that."

"Do I?" He knew his voice was cold and harsh, but his thoughts were in turmoil. He should take her straight to the emergency room—and make sure she wouldn't remember where she'd gotten shot. He could take away her memory and her identification, so nobody would know who she was. But even as he considered that plan, he rejected it.

He couldn't forget the dream. Suppose he was wrong about Caldwell's orchestrating it? Suppose Emma had somehow reached out to him on her own? Or, even more likely, because she had been at Caldwell's enclave and in need of help, and because he himself spent a good deal of time making plans to bring down his old enemy, they had simply found each other. Two people, both isolated, both focused on a common foe—and one with the extrasensory powers that would make a bond between them possible. That the bond had taken such an erotic turn could have been the result of his own long abstinence and, to be completely honest, his loneliness. God knows, he'd been lonely....

Of course, there was one other question he couldn't answer. He slept during the day, and she presumably slept at night. When had they shared these dreams? It must be early in the morning when she was still sleeping and he had just gone to bed. As Nick debated that question, Emma reached for his hand and clasped it with icy fingers.

"Let me stay," she whispered. "If I go to the hospital, he'll...he'll find me. He'll send someone...like he sent Frazier to my hotel this morning."

Nick pulled his hand from hers. "If he found you at your hotel, how do you know he hasn't followed you here?"

"I made sure..." She tried to reach for him, then flopped back against the sofa, a spasm of pain crossing her features.

The pain tipped the balance for him. Her anguish reminded him of his own humanity. Or maybe he was simply unable to bear seeing the woman to whom his subconscious self had been making love only a few hours ago experience anything but pleasure.

She might be a spy. And she might not be. But she surely was injured and in need of help. And he was going to help her. Later, he could probe for the truth.

"I'll take a look at the wound," he said, his voice coming out more roughly than he'd intended.

She let out a small sigh.

"I'll be right back."

He strode to the bathroom, where he kept clean towels, and brought one back. When he slid it under her upper body, she whimpered, though she quickly stifled the sound.

"Sorry."

"That's okay."

It wasn't okay. Once again he focused his mind on hers, using his power to put her into a light trance, reaching out to her the way he would if he were going to drink from her—which he wasn't, he told himself firmly. He was just easing her pain.

Her shoulder bag was still slung across her chest. He eased it up and over her head and set it on the floor. Then, trying to still the slight trembling in his fingers, he began to roll up her T-shirt.

In his dreams—their dreams—she'd been naked under the gown she'd been wearing. He let out a sigh of relief when he discovered she was wearing a bra. Lacy and not entirely opaque as it was, it nevertheless covered the essentials and helped him to stay focused on her wound, not her breasts.

"Am I hurting you?" he asked.

"No," she said dreamily. He knew she would be feeling as if she were drifting on a fuzzy cloud. "I like your voice," she murmured. "Are you from England?"

"Yes," he answered absently. He could see where the bullet had entered, between her ribs. Rolling her to the side, he noted that the slug had exited through her back.

He was no doctor, but he had seen his share of serious injuries. And he had talents that medical men didn't possess. Closing his eyes, he stroked his fingers along her skin, feeling the path that the bullet had taken. It had passed between two ribs, nicking both of them, but it had missed her lungs.

Bending forward, he pressed his tongue to the wound, the taste of her blood setting off a buzzing in his brain. He wanted to suck on the wound, to draw from her, but he resisted the temptation, forcing himself only to bathe the injury. His saliva had properties that no ordinary human's possessed. He used it after he drew blood, to heal the punctures made by his fangs. And he had used it in the past to heal far worse injuries than Emma's.

He did that now, ruthlessly shoving aside his own need while he licked the entrance wound first, then the place where the bullet had exited her body. He did it swiftly and efficiently.

But not swiftly enough. The smell of her blood set off a torrent of need inside him. Before he could stop himself, he made small punctures in the pale satin skin over the injured ribs. He took a sip, then another before he could wrench himself away.

Clenching his jaw, he pushed to his feet and took a backward step.

"Sleep," he murmured, his hands trembling badly as he slipped off her shoes.

He went to the linen closet for a blanket and spread it over her. Then he stole out the back door, into the night, to satisfy his raging thirst.

He was still worried about the bikers. He had scared them, but he hadn't wiped their memories. They could come back. He would have to go after them in a little while.

First, though, he had to drink.

It was fully dark. The storm had passed, leaving the sky alight with stars. Nick headed for the woods, senses tuned to the sounds and smells of the forest as he looked for his herd of deer.

The animals were considered a nuisance by many residents of the Baltimore-Washington suburbs. They might be beautiful to look at, but they chomped the greenery and flowers in people's gardens, leaped out onto the roads to collide with vehicles and served as hosts for ticks that spread Lyme disease. Most people tried every way they could think of to keep the creatures away from their yards. He, on the other hand, had planted a garden designed to attract them.

As he sensed the herd's presence, he sent them calming thoughts, making his way almost silently through the trees toward them. It wasn't like communicating with humans, of course. But the animals had learned to anticipate his moving among them, and they stilled as he approached.

He selected a doe that he hadn't used in several weeks, speaking gently to her and stroking her stiff coat. Then he lowered his head, murmuring to her as his fangs slid from their sheaths. He tipped back her head, holding it in place so he could sink the fangs into her neck and draw her blood. Not enough to drain her—he'd learned long ago to control his urge to kill. He took only enough to satisfy his thirst, enjoying the gamy tang of her blood.

When he had taken what he needed, he stepped away from the doe. She looked at him with huge brown eyes, blinking as if she were coming out of a trance.

"Thank you," he said. "Now, go back to your friends." To speed her on her way, he gave her a pat on the rump.

She bounded off, and he watched her disappear into the foliage. Deer blood was never as satisfying as the blood that ran in human veins, but it kept him alive.

As he made his way back through the woods to his house, he thought about the problem of Emma Birmingham. Again, the question arose in his mind: Had Caldwell sent her to spy on him?

There was another possibility, too, one that would be even harder to determine: The monster might have sent her without her knowing it. Caldwell could have tampered with her mind, then launched her like a guided missile, set to explode when the time was right. That would be a hell of a note. But it wasn't beyond the scope of the Master's powers.

Caldwell, as he was calling himself now, had been on this earth for more than six hundred years, and in that time he had achieved what few vampires ever did: He had learned to tolerate sunlight. He had also made the manipulation of human beings a science, as Nick knew from first-hand experience. He had been under Caldwell's sway for a time, nearly half a year, until he had finally realized the extent of the man's evil nature.

He'd escaped the Master's coven in France— not unscathed, not even human anymore, thanks to the Master's error of making him one of the undead. But he had escaped, and he had been dogging the rotter's heels ever since. He wouldn't be satisfied until Caldwell was destroyed.

And Caldwell knew it.

Suppose the Master had decided on a preemptive strike, in the lovely form of Emma Birmingham? It would be just like him to use a woman for such a purpose.

Nick strode into the house, aware that time was ticking by. He had to get back to the bikers. But first he checked on Emma.

She was sleeping soundly, and he took the opportunity to rifle through her leather purse. Her driver's license said she was Emma Birmingham. So did her credit cards and her library card. The documents all indicated that she lived in Manitou Springs, Colorado. The IDs might all have been forgeries. Caldwell surely could have provided good ones. But at least on the surface they appeared genuine, even to his practiced, private investigator's eye.

She stirred, and he shoved the things back into her bag, then knelt beside her.

"Nicholas?"

His chest tightened when she spoke his name. She should be sleeping, but she'd managed to struggle back to consciousness. Taking advantage of her drugged-like state, he questioned her again.

"Why did you come here?"

Her word were slurred as she replied, "I need your help."

"Who are you working for?"

"No one. My sister...Margaret."

"How did you find me?"

She started to answer, her eyelids flickering open briefly. But she made only a few soft, incoherent sounds, then fell silent. He didn't press her further. She needed to heal before they talked.

"Go back to sleep," he murmured, then went to the medicine cabinet and fetched sterile gauze and surgical tape—two of the many props he'd bought in case an occasion arose where his house had to appear normal to an outsider. There were similar items scattered throughout the place, things ordinary people used all the time but that he himself would never have need of.

Carefully, he dressed Emma's wound before

going upstairs to prepare a bedchamber for her. After carrying her upstairs and settling her in bed, he gave her silent orders to stay asleep.

Outside, he used a detergent and solvent mixture to wash away the gasoline from the foundation of his house. Finding the keys still in the ignition, he drove Emma's rental car to a small clearing behind the house, where nobody was likely to see it. Then he descended to the basement, his thoughts turning to the problem of the bikers.

He went to the locked dressing room where he kept his disguises, since it was often convenient for him to masquerade as an entirely different person. Digging around, he found a shaggy wig that made him look like a Woodstock refugee. After applying some makeup to give himself a few wrinkles, he added a pair of windowpane glasses to the look. Finally, he changed into faded jeans and a plaid shirt.

In the garage, he selected a Toyota Corolla—a small car that shouldn't draw any notice—opened the secret door and drove up the steeply angled ramp, heading for the bar where he knew the Ten Oaks gang hung out.

He had to repress a wave of disgust when he stepped inside the place. It was a pigsty—thanks to the presence of Butch McCard and his friends.

They were all there, getting drunk as usual, including the guy whose fingers he'd mangled with his boot heel. The moron was probably too drunk on cheap gin to feel the pain.

Nick approached the bar and ordered a beer. When the bartender handed it to him, he stuck his tongue in the mouth of the bottle while he pretended to take a swig. As he carried the bottle to a table, he managed to pour some of the brew into a couple of empty glasses, shielding the action with his body.

He sat down at a corner table, his back to the wall. With his vampiric hearing capabilities, he had no trouble listening to the biker's conversation.

"Dude, are you okay?"

"My head hurts."

"That bastard. He's got, like, jet engines on his feet or something."

"And jackhammers for fists."

"Yeah. We should go back and finish the job— burn his house down, like we was gonna do."

"Naah, he's a menace, dude. We gotta be careful."

"What about the girl? We gonna get in trouble for that?"

"She don't know who we are."

"But what about the freak? Suppose he comes after us."

Nick had heard enough. Keeping his head down, he sent his thoughts flying toward them.

*You don't remember what happened this afternoon. You went to a man's house, but you don't remember why or how to get there. You don't remember who he was. You don't remember that anyone was with him. But you do remember you want to keep away from the guy. Because something really bad will happen if you tangle with him again.*

He leaned back in his seat, waiting to make sure the message had gotten through.

He didn't have long to wait.

"Are you okay, dude?" one of them said.

"My head hurts."

"Something bad happened to me, but...I can't remember."

"Wasn't we ambushed?"

"Uh...something...."

"Wait a minute. Didn't it have to do with...with..."

Nick smiled to himself as he left the bar. The Ten Oaks gang was under control. They wouldn't be back to bother him again.

He hurried to his car and drove out of the parking lot, onto the road that would lead him home. When he was sure nobody was following him, he yanked the wig off of his head, relieved to be rid of the hot, itchy thing.

His thoughts were once more focused on Emma Birmingham and what to do about her.

Nobody else had ever spent the night—or the day—at his house. But she was going to have to rest and regain her strength. He couldn't simply turn her out. If she was telling the truth and Caldwell found her…Nick knew what the consequences would be for Emma, and he knew he wouldn't be able to live with himself if he threw her to the wolves.

Yet allowing her to stay at his place, having her so close, could rapidly become intolerable for him—and downright dangerous for her. She had aroused him in his dreams, and now the flesh-and-blood woman was lying in one of his bedrooms. He wanted her—badly—and he didn't know how long he would be able to resist her. Deer blood was perfectly sufficient for his needs, but it was like a steady diet of beer when he craved champagne.

Emma was the very finest champagne. And he was dying of thirst.

Sighing, he weighed the choices and came to the conclusion that there was only one. He would have to keep Emma at home, with him.

He hoped he could keep his hands—and all the rest of his body parts that wanted her—under control. But he feared the hope was futile.

DAMIEN CALDWELL struggled to contain his rage. He'd lost Emma Birmingham. Frazier and the rest of the incompetents he'd sent after her had let her slip through their grasp. In doing so, they'd failed him, and he took such failure very personally.

He'd been born into an age when most of the population lived in hovels, toiled in the fields for harsh masters and died before they were thirty. He'd started out as one of those sniveling wretches.

Then a group of vampires had taken up residence in a desert fortress near his home. They'd captured a dozen local youths, including him, to use as servants—and as food. But Felora, one of the women, had taken a fancy to Ali, as he was called then. She'd invited him to her bed, where she'd taught him sexual secrets he'd never even dreamed of.

He eventually would have died from blood loss, but when he was bitten by a poisonous snake, Felora had realized that she wasn't willing to give him up. To save his life, she'd turned him into one of her kind, without asking permission of her master.

Kahlile, the vampire master, had found out and killed her. He would have killed Ali, too, but while the Master was focused on Felora, Ali had escaped.

He'd managed to join a caravan heading across the desert. Only a few of the travelers made it to their destination alive. Ali fed off them, killing many. As soon as they neared civilization, they fled, leaving the wealth of the caravan to Ali. He sold the goods and purchased a luxurious residence in Baghdad. He had then proceeded to gather as much wealth as possible, for he had long since learned that great wealth gave one great power. And he had made a vow to himself that he would never again be vulnerable to any human being—man or woman.

Over the years he'd carefully changed his speech patterns and his appearance to conform to the age and the country where he was living, but he had seen no reason to change his way of life. He was a student of psychology and mind control and a whole host of mental disciplines. That knowledge and his vampire powers had given him absolute control over his followers.

Yet he'd sent his slaves to do a simple job, and they had failed him.

Using miracles of technology, the computer and the cell phone, as well as his hacking skills, he had tracked Emma Birmingham to a hotel in Baltimore, an ATM in the inner harbor, a car rental firm at BWI airport, a gun shop in Elkridge and a Wal-Mart in Ellicott City. It should have been easy to waylay her in any one of those places, especially the airport where he had stationed several slaves, thinking she might try to get a flight home to Colorado. But no. Frazier,

Findlay, Briggs…she had eluded all of them. They had spent an entire day running after her, calling him each time they failed, expecting him to tell them how to do their jobs, as if he hadn't already done that.

And now the beautiful and sly Ms. Birmingham had vanished. She'd been missing for over twenty-four hours, and the trail was growing colder by the minute.

In frustration, Damien ran a hand through his hair. He felt anger building inside his skull, giving him the mother of all headaches. He made more phone calls, barked orders. But still his head pounded.

Well, he knew how to soothe himself. He thought about his herd of prime female flesh.

Pressing a button on his phone, he waited for Leroy Putnam to come into the office. Men and women at the Refuge had very different duties. Only men became guards and his personal assistants.

"Yes, sir?" Putnam asked, stepping into the office and closing the door behind him.

"I want to hold a special ceremony tonight."

"Yes, sir."

"Gather the inner circle, and have them ready to go to the amphitheater at midnight."

"Yes, sir." Putnam licked his lips nervously. "Who is going to be the sacrifice?"

He made his slave wait while he thought about the women, evaluating their good and bad points, and deciding who among them he could do without. Finally he named a short plump brunette who held limited sexual appeal and who, frankly, bored him. Still, she would perform one final service for him.

When he announced her name, Putnam visibly relaxed, obviously glad that he wasn't scheduled to die tonight.

Damien rarely killed men these days. He much preferred the blood of women because he craved the extra edge of their sexuality flowing into his body. But he sacrificed a man every once in a while because it helped keep the males in line. It was always someone who displeased him. Someone who had failed to carry out his orders.

He gave instructions to Putnam. "Have her bathed and dressed in the traditional white robes."

"Yes, sir."

"Then put her in the holding cell."

Headache abating, he felt much calmer than he had a few minutes ago. He smiled as he anticipated the pleasure that was to come.

## Chapter Five

Emma struggled toward consciousness, but
somehow it was impossible to break through the
final barrier. She was asleep and yet she wasn't.

Her head felt muzzy. Like the time her boyfriend Barry had stolen some of that designer
drug from his brother and given it to her. It had
made her sick, and Margaret had taken care of her.
Margaret always knew what to do. Margaret
would help her…. Margaret would…

*Margaret!*

Emma fought desperately to wake up as
memory drifted back to her. Margaret was in
trouble, in terrible danger. She had to help her,
rescue her…. But she couldn't wake up.

What was wrong with her? Was she drugged?
But, no, she knew the man wouldn't have given
her anything that would hurt her.

Man. What man?

Oh, yes. The man she'd found in her dreams.

Lovely dreams. Maybe he was there now, waiting for her. She could try to find him again and…

Suddenly, memory floated back, and she remembered that she didn't need to dream to find him. She was in his house, and he was real. He had saved her from…something.

His name. She needed to remember his name.

"Nicholas Vickers," a deep voice said, and she knew he was standing beside her.

Her eyelids fluttered open. He was bending over her, brushing back her hair.

She blinked at him. When he took a quick step backward, her gaze followed, widening her perspective on her surroundings. She was in a large bedroom filled with polished antiques and rich fabrics. The bedsheets were like a flower garden. She moved her head against the pillow, letting her mind drift, simply wanting to be alive in this place.

Then frightening memories intruded, and her gaze snapped back to the darkly handsome Nicholas Vickers.

"That guy in the leather jacket," she breathed. "He shot me."

"And you wouldn't let me take you to the hospital," Vickers supplied, his tone disapproving.

"Because of Caldwell."

His expression turned stony, and she looked away. Shifting on the bed, she reached down to touch the wound over her ribs. It was covered with a light bandage, but she felt no pain below the gauze. No pain at all. Impossible. Unless…

Her gaze flew back to his. "How long have I been here? What day is this?"

"The day after you arrived," Vickers replied.

She frowned. "But my side doesn't hurt. I mean…"

"You're young and healthy, and you obviously heal fast."

"From a bullet wound?"

"It seems so," he said easily, yet his gaze shifted away from her.

She studied him carefully, certain he was hiding something. "Do you have some magic healing potion?"

He gave her a negligent shrug. "Perhaps."

Clearly, she wasn't going to get a real answer out of him, not about her injury, anyway.

"Tell me about those guys in leather jackets," she said. "The ones who were trying to burn down your house. Do they have something against you?"

"Actually, they do. A local homeowner's association hired me to eject them from a graveyard they'd been defiling."

"So they decided to retaliate," she concluded.

"It would appear so. But they didn't succeed— and I do most sincerely appreciate your brave efforts to save my humble home."

She felt heat rising in her cheeks. "Well, I wasn't going to just sit there and watch them set your house on fire."

"Nevertheless, I thank you." He paused briefly, then said, "The problem is, I don't know how they found me. Or even know how they figured out who crashed their graveside party. I didn't exactly leave them a calling card."

"You think somebody told them who you were and where you live?"

"Like who?" he shot back. His gaze was riveted to her face, as if he honestly expected her to know the answer.

She shrugged. "I have no idea."

His eyes narrowed, and he studied her a moment longer. She had the strange feeling that he was weighing her fate in the balance. Then, abruptly, his whole demeanor changed—for the better. "You need to eat," he said, sitting down beside her on the bed and picking up a mug from the nightstand.

He handed it to her, and she pushed herself into a sitting position before taking it from him. The mug held warm chicken soup. Canned. But then, how many guys would go to the trouble of making chicken soup from scratch, or even know how to do it? That had certainly been beyond her mother's skills.

She took a few sips under his watchful gaze.

When the mug was half-empty, she said, "That's enough for now."

He lifted the mug from her hands and set it on the bedside table, but he didn't stand up or give any indication that he was ready to leave.

She looked at him, and he returned the look, their gazes holding for a long silent moment. Then, slowly, he raised his hand and stroked her hair, his fingers trailing across her cheek, then down her neck. His touch was like a magic wand, instantly relaxing her.

Yet even in her weakened state, she felt the undercurrent of arousal between them, and his expression told her that she wasn't the only one caught in the web of sensuality. What shocked her, though, was the look of aching longing in his eyes. Had any man ever looked at her that way? To her own mind, she was the one who always wanted too much—or, at least, wanted more than the men she'd known had been able or willing to give. That she had such an effect on this particular man—this near-stranger— was amazing to her. It also gave her an unexpected feeling of power combined with vulnerability.

For the first time in years, she felt her defenses crumbling. She wanted to open herself to Nicholas Vickers in ways that she knew were dangerous. Almost certainly, she would end up hurt, heartbroken. But she didn't want to stop. She wanted...so much.

"I love your accent," she whispered. "You're from England, right?"

"We covered this ground yesterday," he replied with a faint smile.

"Did we? I don't remember."

"You were a little woozy. Yes, I'm from England. But I thought I'd gotten rid of my accent."

"Almost, but not quite. It's sexy." Before her rational self could take over, she said, "Would you please…"

"What?"

"I'd like you to lie down with me."

His entire body went rigid, his features stiffening into a mask. Afraid he'd been offended by her forwardness, she rushed on. "There's something I have to find out about…about us. I hadn't met you until yesterday, but I dreamed about you."

He remained rock-still, but his gaze was hotly intense, locked with hers. "Why?" he asked.

"I don't know." She took her lip between her teeth. "Nothing like this has ever happened to me. I mean, there's been the thing Margaret, my sister, and I have between us because we're twins—not telepathy or anything like that. Just a sort of sixth sense about each other. But I've never had any imaginary friends or had dreams about somebody I never met, then found out he was—" her voice trailed off to a whisper "—that he was real."

Swallowing embarrassment, ignoring her fear

of being hurt in a way she'd never been hurt before, she said, "I have to know. I just have to find out if kissing you for real is the same as it was in the dream." And before she could change her mind, she cupped her hand around the back of his neck and tugged him toward her.

ASTONISHED beyond speech, Nicholas resisted the gentle pressure of Emma's hand pulling him toward her. He prided himself on being able to control his feelings. Such control had been hard-won, a matter of survival. But he'd been holding back for so long that he barely remembered how it felt to reveal all of himself to another person.

Except in the dreams. His subconscious self had held back nothing in those erotic encounters with Emma. He knew all the intense passion of which he was capable had been fully revealed.

And she was asking him to repeat the experience, for real.

Of course, she didn't know that he, too, had experienced the dreams. He very deliberately hadn't told her. He didn't know how it had happened, hadn't known such a thing was even possible. But having had a preview of what lovemaking with Emma would be like, he simply didn't have it in him to resist.

Just for a moment, he told himself, letting her draw him toward her. Just one kiss…

His lips met hers, softly, sweetly. But within the space of a heartbeat, the balance shifted. The kiss went from sweet to steamy in seconds. And it was better than any dream he'd ever had. Richer, full of textures and layers that begged to be explored.

He was good at kissing, a connoisseur, having had a very long time to practice the art form. He applied himself wholly to sharing his experience with Emma. He dipped his tongue into her mouth, sliding it sensually against hers. He nibbled and sucked on her full lower lip. He widened his mouth to cover hers completely, angling his head for the deepest possible contact—and she gave it to him, surrendering her mouth to his totally.

Yet he wanted more. So much more.

Something was drawing him to this woman, something he didn't understand. He'd met her only yesterday, yet he felt as though he had known her for months...years. Her mouth was familiar to him, moving hungrily against his. The sounds of her arousal—small, low, throaty noises—were ones he'd heard before. And it all felt so completely right.

When she fumbled for his hand and brought it to her breast, he made a strangled sound, wave after wave of heat washing through him. He held the soft, supple mound, his fingers stroking the hardened tip. Blood pounded in his head and in his loins, and it felt wonderful and...dangerous.

Far too dangerous.

Breaking the kiss, he removed his tingling hand from her breast.

"Don't stop," she protested, her breath coming hard and fast.

He didn't even attempt to keep his voice steady. "This cannot be good for you. For God's sake, a bullet went through your body only yesterday. You need to heal."

She answered with a small nod, and he breathed out a sigh of both relief and acute disappointment. Both sentiments, however, were short-lived.

"Then lie down with me," she said. "I'll heal much better if you hold me close."

He would have liked nothing better. But one of them had to think rationally, and it seemed he had been elected.

"That would not be a good idea," he said, hearing the thickness in his own voice.

"I know you won't do anything I don't like."

He laughed. "Trouble is, you've made it very clear what you'd like."

A blush reddened her cheeks. "Because you've woven a spell around me."

He tipped his head to one side. "Is that what you really think?"

She gave a small shrug. "It's like Damien Caldwell. He wove a spell over a lot of people, my sister included."

A bolt of anger flashed through him. "I'll thank you not to compare me to that bastard."

"I just meant…" She hesitated, then started again. "I'm sorry. I know you're different."

"How?" he asked. "Tell me how you know that."

"Caldwell wants to hurt people, to control them," she whispered. "I know you mean me no harm."

Nick wasn't so sure that was true, but he kept the observation to himself. While he was deciding what to say, she reached for his hand and tugged. "Please. I want to feel you next to me."

"I told you, that isn't a good idea," he answered.

"You want to," she murmured.

"We can't always have what we want." Still, he thought, getting closer to her might be useful. Maybe he could get some information out of her. He hesitated, knowing very well that he was rationalizing.

*The hell with it,* he thought, kicking off his shoes, then settling down beside her on the bed.

"I'd rather have you under the covers," she said softly.

He turned his head toward her. "I think it's safer if I stay topside."

She gave a small sigh.

It had been a long time since he'd lain in bed with a woman. As bad an idea as he knew it was, he wanted to enjoy it for a little while. Then he'd ask his questions. When she closed her eyes, he did, too. An instant later, they snapped open at the feel of her fingers slipping under his shirt and her small hand flattening against his chest.

If her action hadn't already jolted him back to reality, her next words would have.

"Tell me what happened between you and Caldwell."

He pushed up on one elbow and looked down at her. "And just how do you know that anything happened between us?"

"I sneaked into his office and went through some of the papers in his filing cabinets."

"You *what?*" Aghast, Nick gaped at her. "Do you have any idea how dangerous that was?"

She looked defiant. "I had to. I was looking for something I could use against him—anything that might help me get my sister away from that place. I found a file on you."

"Bloody hell!"

"He hates you," Emma continued. "And you obviously hate him. What happened?"

He didn't owe her any explanations, but the inexplicable bond between them compelled him to answer her question, made him want to share everything with her. He *wanted* to tell her, in a way he hadn't wanted to tell anyone anything in a very long while.

"I was one of the Master's followers," he said flatly.

She sucked in a sharp breath.

"It ended badly."

"You were…one of his inner circle?" she pressed.

He felt his face contort. "Yes. It makes me sick to think about it now, but, yes, I was one of the men he trusted."

Emma laid a hand over his. "He messes with people's minds. He messed with yours. Just thank God you got away."

Nick answered with a tight nod. "Yes, he was always a persuasive bastard. But at that time he treated his inner circle more like equals—not as he does now, at the Refuge."

"You weren't at the Refuge?" she asked in surprise.

"No. He's gathered groups of people around him in many different places. He stays until things get too dangerous—until, for instance, someone with power and influence raises a fuss about a missing daughter or son, or something like that. Then he clears out, goes someplace else and starts over. When I met him, he lived in France."

"So…" She shifted under the covers, burrowing closer to him. "How did you happen to meet him?"

"At a party in Cannes. A long time ago, I was one of the…beautiful people."

She gave him a puzzled frown. "You were a Hollywood producer or something?"

Nick laughed. "No, my father was a duke."

Her jaw actually dropped. "You're kidding!"

"Afraid not."

"What's your family name?"

He gave her one of the lines he'd been using for years when he talked about his background. "Since I'm an embarrassment to my family, I'd rather keep that to myself."

"An embarrassment? Why?"

"Well, in their social circles, one doesn't brag about a son who works as a private detective. One prays that no one finds out."

"Oh. But that's so unfair!"

"In any case," he continued, "I was the third son, not first in line to inherit the title. But I had plenty of money, and I was never going to have to work for a living. I was…well, quite frankly, shallow. I spent my time traveling and going to parties. I heard about Caldwell from a friend, and I thought he sounded intriguing. So I asked for an invitation to a ball I knew he'd be attending."

Nick didn't describe the glittering occasion, with the hall illuminated by huge candlelit chandeliers and the men and women dressed in silks and satins. He let her form her own picture of the event, which he thought probably resembled a presidential inauguration gala or an Oscar-night party filled with movie stars decked out for the red carpet.

Smiling to himself despite the pain the memories evoked, he continued. "I got into a conversation with Caldwell at the ball. His ideas sounded intelligent. He made me believe that he cared about my welfare. And I thought I could learn from him. I moved into his—" Nick stopped on the verge of saying "castle" and instead said, "estate. While I was there, I fell in love with one of the women he had gathered around him."

"And she loved you?" Emma asked quietly.

He lifted one shoulder in a shrug. "I thought so."

"Then it's very different from the way he operates now. At the Refuge, nobody gets involved with anyone but him."

Nick gave a harsh laugh. "I suspect I have a good deal to do with his having adopted that policy. Jeanette did return my feelings, but then she changed. She became enthralled with the Master, and I couldn't get through to her anymore, though I tried. Caldwell didn't like my persistence. So to make his point, he used Jeanette in one of his midnight ceremonies. Do you know what that means?"

Beside him, Emma's body had gone rigid. "He killed her?" she breathed.

"Yes."

She looked at him, her huge blue eyes wide and full of sadness. "You didn't know about the ceremonies before that?"

He had known. In the months after Caldwell had made him a vampire, he had taken part in some of the fun and games. He had been brought up to see himself as superior to ninety-nine percent of the world's population. And with his new vampiric values—which was to say, viewing mortals as little more than food—he had thought of the women Caldwell killed as necessary sacrifices. A shame they had to die, but, well, *c'est la vie*.

Jeanette had opened his eyes to the truth. She'd been so sweet, so innocent, so idealistic. And she'd been the low-born daughter of a shipping merchant, a nobody, not a woman he likely would have met, much less loved, if he'd remained at home in England.

When the Master had begun to focus on her, Nick had been horrified. He had known what would happen, and he was powerless to prevent it. In the end, he was forced to stand by and watch her be corrupted. And as he'd observed the Master at work, seducing the woman he loved, preparing her for the final sacrifice, he'd begun to see his own life, his own ethics and morals, quite differently.

When the Master killed Jeanette, Nick had gone mad and fought his former mentor. Caldwell had won. He'd drained Nick of blood and left him for dead. But he'd miscalculated. Nick recalled the agony of lying on the stone floor of the castle dungeon, so weak he could barely open his eyelids. But he hadn't been entirely gone. When one of the slaves had come to take his body away, he'd drawn enough blood from the man to revive himself and escape.

There was no way he could tell the details of that sordid story to Emma. And no way he could explain his radical transformation to her.

All at once, he felt trapped in a conversation that he should never have started. He'd climbed into bed with her intending to pump her for information about Caldwell and the Refuge, and he'd ended up saying too much about himself—and thinking too much about his own repellent past. Big mistake.

Emma was staring at him, still waiting for his answer to her question. A lie sprang into his mind, but he found he couldn't get it past his lips. And since he couldn't tell her the truth, either, he took the coward's way out. He used his powers on her again, making her eyelids flutter closed.

Really, he was doing her a favor, he told himself. She needed to rest.

When she lay back against the pillow, he felt some of the tightness in his chest ease. She had asked him to lie in bed with her, and now that she was sleeping, he allowed himself the luxury of holding her in his arms, stroking his lips against her cheek, then her neck.

His whole body throbbed. He wanted to tip her head back and sink his fangs into her. Because he had tasted her blood when he had healed her wound, he already knew how sweet she would be.

He clenched his jaw to stop himself from doing what he knew he'd regret. She had already lost blood, and her body needed time to make more. Drinking from her would be a crime. But the need for her made the slits that sheathed his fangs ache. And the erection straining against the front of his jeans made him want to rip them off, wake Emma and make wild, passionate love to her.

He knew that if he took that fateful step, there would be no going back. He would want more. For a vampire, sex without the drawing of blood was like sex without orgasm—pleasurable, a way to feel close to another person, but not truly satisfying. With someone he wanted deeply, as he wanted Emma, it would be supremely frustrating to stop short of what his vampiric nature drove him to crave.

He knew intuitively that if he started with Emma, he'd want more. He wanted to come inside her and, as he did, to sink his teeth into her flesh and drink from her. And doing so would be the beginning of the end. Because he couldn't tell her what he was. Nor could he make love to her over and over, each time blocking her memory of what happened at the end. More than that, he couldn't drink from her repeatedly without threatening her life.

So their relationship would end as all the others he'd tried to have had ended, with him back where he'd started—utterly alone.

Nick allowed himself a few more minutes of torture, holding Emma in his arms. Finally, when he felt as though he would explode if he didn't sink his teeth into her slender neck, he climbed out of bed, settled the covers around her again and picked up the shoes he had discarded.

Going downstairs to his closet, he changed into clean jeans and a T-shirt, then hopped into his Mercedes and headed to the grocery store. Emma would need more food when she awoke.

A STAKEOUT was the most boring activity Trailblazer could imagine. But he was being compensated well for the long hours of sitting in his car, waiting and watching.

The wait was suddenly over as Nicholas Vickers drove past on the country lane leading away from his house.

Trailblazer waited for half a minute after the Mercedes sedan sped past. Then he pulled onto the blacktop without turning on his lights and followed Vickers.

They drove past a shopping center with an all-night grocery, then crossed the line into the next county.

Four miles down the road, Vickers's Mercedes turned into the parking lot of an upscale watering hole.

As Trailblazer pulled into a parking space at the opposite end of the lot, he watched Vickers get out of his car and stride toward the door.

So was he here to meet someone? Who?

Trailblazer swallowed. He'd been warned not to get too close to Vickers. But if he waited out here, he wouldn't know who the guy was meeting.

After waiting five minutes, he got out of his vehicle and headed for the door.

NICK HAD LEFT the house thinking he was going to the grocery store to get more food for Emma. But here he was at a bar known for its swinging singles scene. He didn't come to the place often, wanting to maintain his anonymity.

Inside the doorway, he stood with his hands in his pockets, absorbing the feel of the pounding music and the thick atmosphere of sexuality.

Some of the women and men were paired up, but he saw an attractive blonde sitting by herself at a table. Not as attractive as Emma, but she would do.

Their eyes met, and he smiled. Crossing the room, he asked, "Are you looking for company?"

"Uh-huh."

"Can I buy you a drink?"

She studied him with interest. "I'd like that."

"What are you having?"

"A margarita."

He ordered the drink for her and a bottle of Coors for himself. Once again, he faked drinking something besides blood.

"My name's Nick. What's yours?"

"Sandy."

"So what do you do?" he asked.

"I'm a personal trainer."

He had learned how to make small talk with a woman and draw her into his web. "Mmm. I could probably use a few pointers on my workout."

She laughed. "You look like you're already pretty buff."

"A guy can always pick up tips from a good instructor."

But he didn't simply rely on charm. As they

chatted, hc silently used his powers of persuasion on her. She might have come here looking for a relationship. Still, in less than an hour, he had her agreeing to go to a motel with him.

He felt the thrill of victory as they headed for her car. But once they were sitting in a darkened corner of the parking lot, he knew he couldn't go through with the whole motel-room scene. He wanted only her body and her blood. Human blood. A woman's blood. His need didn't require a lot of trappings.

After pulling her toward him, he kissed her. Not like he'd kissed Emma. She'd inspired his passion. This woman was a pale substitute. But she would have to do.

To anyone watching, he knew they would look like a couple making out. But when he bent his head, he fogged her mind and sank his fangs into the tender place where her shoulder met her neck. He drank only enough blood to take the edge off the terrible hunger gnawing at him. Then he healed the wounds, kissed her gently again and wiped the memory of the encounter from her mind.

ACROSS THE PARKING LOT, Trailblazer leaned forward, his gaze fastened on the couple in the car. Vickers certainly had some interesting powers of persuasion. He'd been in the bar less than an hour before he'd come out with this babe.

They'd gone out to her car, but they hadn't driven away. Were they going to have a quickie in the parking lot?

No such luck, Trailblazer realized as Vickers climbed out of the car, went to his own vehicle and drove away.

Had the babe told him to get lost? Or had he just changed his mind?

And where was he going?

Back to the shopping center he'd passed on the way, apparently.

NICK PULLED INTO the parking lot of the local strip mall that had an all-night supermarket. On the way back from the biker bar, he'd grabbed a couple of cans of soup for Emma, but he realized he needed additional provisions.

Since he didn't eat conventional food, he hadn't thought much about it in years. As he walked up and down the aisles, he remembered the dishes he'd loved as a boy. Plum pudding on Christmas, leg of lamb, the cinnamon buns Cook had baked for breakfast.

He picked up a package of something the bakery department called cinnamon buns. They didn't look much like the perfect little gems Cook had made, but maybe Emma would enjoy them.

He bought some frozen dinners and micro-waveable sandwiches called Hot Pockets that he'd seen advertised on television. Adding some fruit to his cart, he recalled the oranges his father had imported from Italy and the apples that had come from their orchard.

Thinking of his long-ago home made him sad. He'd told Emma that his father had been a duke. He hadn't told her that his entire family had been dead for more than fifty years. The influenza epidemic of 1917, World War I and World War II had taken care of them.

After paying for the food, he strode to his Mercedes and pulled out of the lot. A black sedan was behind him, but when he sped up, the other vehicle dropped back.

He relaxed, glad he didn't have to field yet another problem today.

ALEX SHANE checked his watch. He'd gone back to his stakeout, across the river from the Refuge, but nothing interesting had happened in the past few hours. It was almost midnight. Maybe he should pack it in.

He was just about to head home when he saw something that made the hairs on the back of his neck stand up. A group of Caldwell's followers had emerged from the mansion, clad in white, walking as if in a procession. Moving silently along the riverbank, they turned toward a grove of trees.

Alex knew there was an amphitheater in the grove, where Caldwell carried out some sort of pagan ceremonies. He'd sneaked up on the place once but had barely gotten away without being caught by a suspicious guard carrying an Uzi. After that, he'd stayed on his side of the river, knowing Sara would never forgive him if he made her a widow.

He scanned the line of men with his night-vision binoculars. They had a woman with them. Her hands appeared to be tied behind her back, and she was stumbling as though she'd been drugged.

Soon the trees swallowed the weird procession. For long moments Alex strained to see anything more. He thought he heard chanting, like a chorus of many male voices. Then silence reigned again until, suddenly, it was pierced by a terrible scream. Then nothing.

Alex waited, every muscle in his body taut. Should he row across the damn river, risk getting shot?

The men came out of the woods soon thereafter. The woman was nowhere to be seen.

Feeling sick and impotent, he went home to Sara, Beth and Jack.

After a couple of hours of quality time with his wife, he left her with a satisfied smile on her face and went down to his office to call Light Street. He wanted to see if they could get a line on Nicholas Vickers.

## Chapter Six

Before pulling into the garage, Nick took the time to search Emma's car. He didn't find anything incriminating, which proved nothing. But he did see that she'd purchased some clothing to replace what she'd presumably left at the Refuge. So he carried the bag into the house.

Then he stood for a long time under the shower, washing off the scent of the woman named Sandy.

Finally, when he couldn't stay away from Emma any longer, he carried the bag of clothing upstairs and set it on her dresser. Then he sat in a chair in a corner of her room and watched her sleep, admiring the slope of her nose, the curve of her lips, the tendrils of blond hair around her face. From across the room, he listened to the sound of her breathing—in and out in a steady rhythm.

When the rhythm changed, he tensed.

She opened her eyes and blinked, obviously trying to orient herself. Then her gaze shot to him.

"Nick? Have you been here the whole time?"

"No. I went grocery shopping," he answered, leaving out the part of the evening he didn't want to talk about.

She moved restlessly in the bed.

"What's wrong?"

Her cheeks took on a bit more color. "I have to go to the bathroom."

"Let me help you get up."

The moment he touched her, he was aroused all over again. So much for being sated after his brief interlude with another woman.

Trying not to give away his churning emotions, he raised Emma to a sitting position, then helped her stand, noting that she wasn't entirely steady on her legs. But she was in fantastically better shape than she had any right to be—thanks to the treatment he'd given her.

He waited outside the bathroom, then helped her back to bed, vividly aware of her hip brushing against his leg as they made their slow way down the hall.

He'd left a glass of water on the bedside table, and he had to squelch the urge to gulp it down. It would only make him sick.

With a hand that wasn't quite steady, he

handed Emma the glass and waited while she took several sips.

"More soup?" he asked.

"Yes. Thanks. That would be great."

Glad to escape the bedroom, he busied himself in the kitchen, fixing more soup as well as tea and toast.

He returned to her room, set the tray of food on the bedside table, then retreated to the chair in the corner, putting a good eight feet between them.

She ate about half the food, then set down her mug and gave him a direct look. "We need to talk about Caldwell—and the Refuge."

"What about them?"

"I came here because I was hoping you'd help me get my sister out of there. Will you?"

"I don't know."

Her eyes narrowed. "Are you afraid of Caldwell?"

He kept his gaze steady. "You're damn right, I'm afraid of him. I know that blundering into his lair without preparation is a suicide mission. If you escaped from him, you were lucky."

She swallowed. "I know."

"If I'm going to consider going there, we need some ground rules."

"Such as?"

"Neither of us is going to do anything foolhardy. Is that agreed?"

She looked down at her hands, then back at him. "Yes."

He knew she'd mouthed the syllable because she didn't have a choice. He wanted to continue the conversation, but he had run out of time.

Outside, night was turning to the gray light that came before the sunrise, and he felt a tingle along his nerve endings.

It was different for Caldwell. He was old—even for a vampire. He had learned the trick of being able to expose his skin to the sun. But Nick was far behind him in that skill. In an emergency, he could go out during the day—thanks to the modern miracle of heavy sunscreen—but even with protection, two hours was his limit.

And right now he needed to get back to his protected rooms in the basement. He stood, shifting his weight from one foot to the other.

Emma peered at him. "What's wrong?"

"We'll talk later." He started to leave, then forced himself to stay a few more moments to explain a little. "I need to get some shut-eye. I was up most of the night. I sleep in the basement, so don't worry if you don't see me around the house. Make yourself at home. You'll be quite safe."

"Why the basement?" she asked.

"Because I can climate control it best to suit my needs," he said evenly. "But it also has a very effective alarm system, so if you wake up again, don't venture down there. Just be assured that you're safe."

"But what if—"

He cut off the question with the wave of one hand. His head was buzzing now. There were probably more instructions he should give her, but the clawing sensation on his skin had turned to real pain.

As quickly as he could manage, he sent Emma back to sleep, then hurried down to the first floor. His hands were unsteady as he fumbled for his keys, intending to lock the door to his office. But he couldn't fit the key into the slot. And his skin was burning with an unbearable intensity.

Dizzy now, he staggered to the basement stairs, feeling as if he were Superman exposed to Kryptonite. Sunlight was *his* Kryptonite.

Unsteady on his feet, he made it to the blessed darkness of the lower level. He almost forgot to set the alarm, but he remembered it at the last minute before stepping into his private quarters and locking the door behind him.

He dragged off his clothes and fell onto the bed. And for a while he slept like the dead.

EMMA FOUGHT to wake up. After the soup and tea, she needed to go to the bathroom again. But it was difficult to drag herself from sleep. Still, she knew where she was, and the thought of embarrassing herself in Nicholas Vickers's guest bed finally brought her to consciousness. When she'd been seven, her mother had married a man who didn't much like children. She'd been frightened of Charles Walters, and she'd started wetting her bed. He'd been furious that she was messing up his expensive bedding, and that had only made matters worse. Ever since then, she'd had a horror of mortifying herself that way.

Climbing out of bed, she staggered down the hall to the bathroom. After using the toilet, she began heading back to bed.

Nick had told her to sleep. She should do that. But she'd caught a glimpse of herself in the mirror and decided she looked exactly as if she'd been on the run for days. A shower would be good. And some clean clothes. Hadn't he put her purchases on the dresser in the bedroom?

After retrieving the clothing, she undressed, then raised her arm and pulled off the gauze bandaging on her ribs, thinking she should replace the dressing after her shower.

To her amazement, she could barely see where the bullet had gone in or come out. She'd never been shot before, but she was pretty sure that Nick had worked some kind of amazing cure.

That made her think about Damien Caldwell again. He'd done something like that at the

Refuge. One of the men had been fixing the roof and had fallen off. He'd been in terrible pain, and she was sure he'd broken some bones. But instead of calling an ambulance, Caldwell had him brought to the office, where he closed the door and did God knows what to the guy.

Two days later, the man had been good as new.

Nick had confessed to being one of Caldwell's disciples. Had the Master taught him special healing techniques?

She wanted to ask—as soon as she made herself presentable.

No, wait. Nick had said he slept in the basement. And he'd told her not to go down there.

Or was she remembering that wrong?

Confused, she hoped the shower would help clear her head. So she turned on the water, then stepped under the spray. The shower was a luxurious state-of-the-art affair with multiple sprays. It felt wonderful on her body. Like the showers at the spa where she and Margaret had gone once for a sister's weekend. Thinking of Margaret woke her up. She was at Nick's because of her sister and the sooner she could get him to take her back to the Refuge, the better. By the time she'd washed her body and her hair and brushed her teeth, she was feeling better. And she was wide awake.

The clock in her bedroom said it was almost

six-thirty. Her stomach growled, and she decided to go downstairs and get something to eat.

She found the tray Nick had left on the kitchen counter. She washed the dishes, then microwaved another serving of soup. As she sipped it, she looked around his kitchen. He had a can opener and a set of expensive knives but almost no cooking utensils and only a couple of copper pots that looked as if they'd come from a gourmet shop and had never been used.

She peered into the cabinets. They were basically empty, except for a package of cinnamon buns. He had orange juice, milk and ground coffee in the refrigerator, and he'd stuffed the freezer with frozen entrees. Was that all he ever ate?

Maybe he had a pantry somewhere. She wandered a little farther—and indeed found a pantry. However, it held not foodstuffs but firearms. How many weapons did one private investigator need? She shrugged and returned to the kitchen.

She opened the cinnamon buns and munched on one as she leaned against the counter.

The kitchen felt like…like a stage set. She couldn't even find paper napkins. So she ate the pastry carefully as she explored the rest of the first floor.

Like her bedroom, it was furnished with expensive antiques and Oriental rugs and some fascinating knickknacks he'd probably picked up on his travels. Scarabs from Egypt. Delicate china from France and England. Venetian glass bowls. Jade animals and a dragon that looked like it might have come from Thailand.

Being here was so strange. She had dreamed of Nicholas Vickers. And walking through the rooms of his home was like taking a tour of a place she somehow already knew.

It was as if she had stepped from reality back into her dreams. But, no, that wasn't quite right.

She picked up a small glass cat and squeezed her fingers around its curved shape before setting it back on the shelf. The dreams had felt so vivid. But this was the reality of Nick's life.

She had met him, talked to him. She was in his house. But she felt she knew him less, not more, than she had a few nights ago. How could that be?

She made a frustrated sound. She'd built up an image of Nicholas Vickers in her imagination. And in appearance he was actually quite close to what she had expected. But now she was dealing with the flesh-and-blood man, not a fantasy figure—and finding him not quite as cooperative as he had been in her dreams.

In her dreams, she had been so positive he would help her. But at this moment she was pretty sure he could go either way. The fear that he might refuse her made her stomach clench.

She just had to bring him around.

She already knew that he hated Caldwell. That was a good sign. And it was a very good sign that he hadn't simply sent her away. He could have dumped her at a hospital, despite her protests. But he'd taken her in and tended to her himself—and probably better than a harried ER staff would have.

She wanted to know more about the man. And not just because she needed his help. Taking her time, she moved on through the rooms, captivated by the house yet on the lookout for information.

She walked back upstairs and toured the bedrooms. They were all luxurious, as if somebody had taken the time to outfit an upscale bed-and-breakfast. But, except for the one she'd occupied, they all looked as if nobody ever slept there. She admired the furnishings and the views from each room, but the first floor was much more interesting. She headed back downstairs.

To her disappointment, she came across not a single photograph of Nick's family. But she forgot all about that when she came to his library. She felt as if she'd found a treasure trove. Like the furnishings he seemed to favor, many of the books on the floor-to-ceiling shelves were old and valuable. But he also had a huge selection of contemporary novels and nonfiction. Lord, Marg would love it in here!

On a side table was a chessboard set up with beautifully carved ivory and ebony pieces. It looked as if a game was in progress. Was Nick playing both sides, or did he have a partner who visited—or remained stashed in a closet somewhere?

Down the hall from the library she came upon a closed door.

When she opened it, she saw a small office with a desk, file cabinets and a computer.

Standing in the doorway, she scanned the room, her fingers itching to see what they might come up with on his computer or in his files. She wanted badly to learn more about the man, but she stopped herself from snooping. She wanted Nick to trust her, and the best way to achieve that end was to *be* trustworthy.

Besides, while she had no qualms about invading Damien Caldwell's privacy, she'd had a legitimate reason to do so. She had none here— save her own burning curiosity. And she felt an odd sense of loyalty to Nick, this man who'd haunted her dreams.

Those dreams had been so intimate, yet in them she'd never seen his bedroom. And it didn't look as if she would anytime soon, either. Was he keeping her away from that private space on purpose?

After closing the office door, she turned and

walked slowly back to the kitchen. Often the door to the basement was found in the kitchen of a house. But not here. She wandered down another hallway until she came to a closed door.

Opening it, she peered down a flight of steps. The basement. The light from the hallway pierced the darkness just enough to illuminate what looked like the cement floor of a typical storage area. No musty smell, but it was still difficult to believe Nick slept down there when he had so many beautiful rooms to choose from.

She stared into the gloom. Nick had told her not to go to the basement, so she wouldn't. But she was damn well going to ask him some questions when he came back up.

IN HIS DARKENED BEDROOM, a dream grabbed Nick by the throat. He was back in France. He recognized the tapestry hanging on the wall behind the low couch where Jeanette sat. They were talking about René Descartes, the sixteenth-century French philosopher who had uttered the famous phrase, "I think. Therefore I am."

Jeanette had been educated far beyond the expectations of the women of her time. She read both Greek and Latin. She knew the classics. And she loved modern literature and science. She was arguing that Descartes's contributions to physics and mathematics were as important as his philosophical ideas. But Nick won the debate by gathering her into his arms and tumbling her to the pile of pillows on the Oriental carpet, as she giggled happily and pretended to resist.

When he landed atop her, the encounter turned from laughter to kisses, and he was able to bank his mounting passion only with the greatest self-control.

Suddenly a shadow fell upon them. Damien Caldwell was standing over them.

"How dare you?" Damien challenged. "Any woman who lives here is mine," he hissed. And with that he yanked Jeanette up and out of Nick's arms.

Nick grabbed for her.

But Caldwell only laughed as he dragged Jeanette away, down an endless corridor.

His breath coming in great gasps, Nick pounded after them. But somehow he could never catch up. As he ran, his panic grew because he knew the terrible ending of the story.

Jeanette's screams echoed in his ears. Only it was no longer Jeanette. It was Emma being dragged away.

"No!" Nick screamed. "Not Emma. Not her, too."

He struggled to wake up, to make sure Caldwell hadn't broken into his house and seized her.

EMMA WAS STILL STANDING at the top of the stairs when she heard a muffled shout.

"Nick?" she called. "Nick, what's wrong?"

When he didn't answer, goose bumps rose on her arms. What if he was sick or in some kind of trouble? What if, despite his alarm system, someone—the bikers, maybe—had broken in to harm him?

He'd told her not to go to the basement. But this was an emergency.

With one hand firmly on the banister, she turned on the light at the top of the steps and started down. When she reached the bottom, she looked around, trying to figure out where to find Nick. The space looked entirely unfinished, nothing like where someone with a lot of money might sleep. She saw a few closed doors and wondered if a finished suite might lie behind one of them.

"Nick?" she called again.

The light went off, and a bloodcurdling howl split the air, followed by the sound of metal clanking behind her.

Her own scream broke from her lips as she whirled, intent on running back up the stairs. But instead of reaching the steps, she smacked into some sort of barrier.

She frantically felt around in the darkness and realized she was facing a metal gate. She searched for a latch that would open it, but she found nothing. And behind her she now heard heavy footsteps approaching. In her fear she could easily imagine that Frankenstein's monster was after her.

Moaning, she dodged to one side. She'd seen some boxes on the floor; maybe she could hide behind them. But before she reached the hiding place, an eerie green light sprang up before her, a motor whirred and mist or smoke began rising from a corner of the room.

In the darkness, she didn't even know in what direction to run. Maybe she could scale the metal gate.

But before she'd gotten so much as a toehold, a hand clamped down on her shoulder, and she dissolved in terror, her scream ringing in her own ears.

# *Chapter Seven*

"Take it easy. It's me—it's Nick. Take it easy, Emma."

He wrapped her in his arms, but she didn't seem to know who he was and kept struggling.

After the raw emotions of his nightmare, when he'd thought Caldwell was dragging her away, he'd awakened to the sound of her screaming.

And her scream was real. Had Caldwell followed her here, intent on dragging her back to the Refuge and sacrificing her in one of his damn ceremonies?

Was that where his dream had come from?

In a panic, he'd rushed into the front of the basement and found her trapped by the security gate.

"It's okay. Everything's okay," he murmured to her now.

Because his night vision was excellent, he could see the terror on her face.

"Emma, it's Nick. You're okay. Everything's okay."

His voice must have finally penetrated her terror, because she lifted her face toward him. "Nick?"

"Yes. Let's get you out of here."

When she slumped against him, he picked her up and carried her to his bedroom, laid her on the mattress and snapped on a low light.

But the first words out of his mouth were hardly gentle. "I told you not to come down here," he bit out.

She raised wounded eyes toward him. "But I heard you call out. I thought you were in trouble."

He muttered a curse. "I was having **a** damn nightmare."

"It must have been a doozie," she said weakly.

She pushed herself up to search his face. And before he could object, she caught his hand and drew him close, pressing herself against him.

He'd awakened from a nightmare about her abduction to the sound of her very real scream. He had dreamed of Emma Birmingham before he'd even met her, but now she was actually here—in his bedroom—and he was helpless to deny reality. With a sound low in his throat, he gathered her close.

"Nick, I was so scared. For you and for me."

"I know. I'm sorry. It was my fault. You got

tangled up in the security system I told you about. As you saw, it's very effective at—"

"Driving an intruder mad?" she interjected. "I'm afraid your 'security system' has a lot in common with a carnival's house of horrors."

He managed a grating laugh. "I guess that's my twisted sense of humor. I used a few elements from a video game I designed."

"A P.I. who can treat gunshot wounds and design video games? Clearly you're a man of many, many talents."

"Yeah," he said uneasily. "Anyway, I figured anyone who broke in here deserved to get scared spitless before the knockout gas hit them. But I didn't expect *you* to get caught in my amusing technology," he added wryly.

"Knockout gas?"

"Yeah. I turned it off."

"I see why you warned me to stay upstairs."

"But you came charging down here anyway. Because you thought *I* was in trouble."

Nothing could have prepared him for that notion—that she had ignored her own best interests when she'd thought he was in danger. Just as he hadn't been prepared for his reaction when he awoke and thought Caldwell really might have her in his clutches. His nightmare was still fresh in his mind, like a raw wound. He had lost Jeanette, and he had thought he would lose Emma, too.

He tried to tell himself that he barely knew Emma Birmingham. But that hadn't stopped him from getting caught up in his fears for her.

"You're too brave for your own good," he said gruffly.

"I'm not brave. Far from it. But I am a pragmatist, and I do need you."

He knew she'd meant that she needed his help to rescue her sister.

But suddenly it was as if they were sharing a dream again, their lips mere inches apart, their heartbeats loud in his ears. And when she lifted her face, he brought his mouth down to hers.

At first he merely sipped from her, but as his own need skyrocketed, he increased the pressure of his lips on hers.

Her mouth opened under his, and he was intoxicated by its warmth, its texture, its sweetness, all of which he had tasted the day before.

He had never brought anyone to this bedroom, not even in a dream. He could hardly believe Emma was here now—here in his lonely sanctuary from the world. Because no matter how he filled his nights, loneliness was the core of his existence.

His fatal love for Jeanette had taught him that honest relationships would never be possible for him. He couldn't tell anyone what he was; he couldn't allow anyone to get close to him.

But right now, the only thing that mattered was the connection he had made with Emma, first in his dreams and now in reality. It couldn't last, but he swept the pain of future loss from his mind and focused on the woman in his arms.

Delicately, his tongue investigated the softness along the inside of her lips, stroking the sensitive tissue. When small sounds rose in her throat, he felt his heart leap.

He angled his head, melded his mouth to hers and kissed her long and deeply, surprised by how satisfying just that mouth-to-mouth contact could be. His tongue prowled possessively over the ridges of her teeth and the silken interior of her lips. Truly, kissing was all he intended to do. All he should do. But as their kisses became deeper and more intimate still, a kind of desperation took hold of him.

He plundered her sweetness, gratified by the way her breathing accelerated.

Lifting his mouth from hers, he kissed the line of her jaw, working his way downward to the slender column of her neck, the line of her collarbone revealed by the neck of her T-shirt.

As he kissed her there, he pushed up her shirt, then lifted her slightly, sliding his hands under the shirt and fumbling with the catch of her bra.

Obligingly, she leaned forward to give him readier access. As he worked the fastening, he smiled, thinking how much easier modern underwear was to remove than its nineteenth-century equivalents.

Easing her back onto the mattress, he rolled her shirt up to her neck and pushed her bra out of the way. When he saw the sweet mounds of her breasts, his breath caught.

"You are so beautiful," he whispered.

"I'm not. I'm perfectly ordinary," she protested a bit breathlessly.

"Well, your body may be ordinary to you, but I can tell you that you're exquisite."

As he finished the declaration, he lifted her breasts in his hands and pressed his face into the valley between them, turning his head first one way and then the other, inhaling as much of her feminine scent as he could while brushing his fingers over her taut nipples, loving the way they hardened even more for him.

"That feels so good," she gasped.

"Sweet saints, yes."

She blinked up at him, and he realized he'd slipped back into the speech patterns of his young manhood.

"You sound like a poet."

"You make me feel poetic."

With a little smile, he reached down to open the zipper—another nice modern device—of her jeans so he could slip his hand inside. He slid his fingers beneath her silken panties, gliding them through the triangle of hair at the apex of her thighs. Then he dipped lower, slipping into her slick folds.

She pressed upward against his fingers, moving her hips. "Oh, Nick."

Clothing had changed, but not the delights of a woman's body. He turned his head to suckle one pebble-hard nipple, hoping he was making her feel as hot and needy as he was. Taking the other small peak between his thumb and index finger, he tugged it gently, watching her face, seeing how much she liked what he was doing.

"Don't stop," she moaned, her eyes closing as she arched into his intimate caress.

As her hips rocked against his fingers, he felt his fangs slip from their sheaths.

She called his name again, and he stoked her pleasure, urging her toward completion. As he felt her body convulse in his arms, he stayed with her and fueled her orgasm. When he felt her physical sensations begin to ebb, he sent a mental fog into her mind so that he wouldn't hurt her.

Then he turned his face, pressing his fangs into the soft flesh of her neck, drawing precious blood from her—feeding the need that had been building since he'd first taken her into his arms.

It was so good, better than he had dreamed it

could be. He wanted to go on and on, drawing from her while he plunged deeply inside her.

But even as that thought surfaced, he knew that he had already gone too far.

He pulled his teeth from her sweet flesh. He had taken from her. But not enough. Not nearly enough.

He used his tongue to seal the small punctures, then watched her eyes blink open to stare at him, her confusion and uncertainty tearing at him.

"What…what happened?"

"Something good," he whispered, knowing he had carried his own pleasure further than it ever should have gone.

"Was that just me or did you…?"

"Both of us," he answered, unwilling to give her any clarification. He had thought that if he took blood from her without having intercourse, he would slake his need. It hadn't worked out that way. He was still hot and wanting.

Maybe because she was feeling embarrassed about what she'd let him do, she looked away from him and around the room. Like the upper floors, his room was furnished with expensive antiques—except for the high-tech bank of video screens on the wall he'd undraped earlier. He took the opportunity to put a little physical distance between them.

"Your surveillance system?" she asked.

"Yeah. That's how I knew that you and those bikers were outside three days ago."

"Oh."

She gestured toward the upper right-hand screen, which showed the storage area where she'd been trapped. "Why did you wait so long to get me out of there?" she asked.

"Because I was still sleeping. I heard you scream, but at first I thought it was part of the nightmare I was having. It took a few minutes for me to figure out it was real," he answered.

She answered with a small nod, then asked, "Can we go back upstairs now?"

"Yes."

She rose from the bed, straightened her clothing and started toward the door. Then she hesitated.

Climbing out of bed, he walked toward her. "The house of horrors is deactivated now."

He stepped out the door, and she followed him into the unfinished part of the basement. When he saw her shiver, he slung his arm around her shoulders and escorted her across the cement floor and up the steps.

Once upstairs, he cleared his throat and asked, "Did you find everything you needed while I was sleeping?"

"Everything I needed?" she echoed. She scuffed a toe against the Oriental runner. "I took a shower and ate. But you haven't told me whether you're going to the Refuge with me."

"I said I hadn't decided yet, " he muttered. He wasn't feeling very good about himself at the moment. He had allowed his loneliness and lust—and leftover fear from the nightmare—to push him over the edge. But he couldn't tell her the magnitude of the mistake he'd made. He'd been swept away by forces he should have controlled. And once he'd taken her blood, he knew that one taste would never be enough.

For her own protection, he should send her away. Far away from him. Or he might prove even more dangerous than Damien Caldwell. But the pleading look in her eyes made sending her away impossible.

Worse, he knew what would happen if he did. Despite his warning, she'd rushed down to the basement because she thought he—practically a stranger—was in danger. Obviously she'd rush back to the Refuge to save her twin sister on her own if he didn't agree to go with her.

That certainty made him want to lock the doors and hold her captive. Which created yet another problem. Could he keep his distance from her while he made plans for an assault on Caldwell's estate?

Struggling for calm, he dragged in a breath and let it out. Reminding her that she'd been shot a few days ago, he said, "You need to rest and heal—while I consider a plan."

He could see she wanted to argue for haste, but she managed to remain silent. And somehow that was worse. She was trying to be cooperative, and he would rather have her at odds with him, so he'd have an excuse to keep her at arm's length.

"Could you just answer one question?" she asked in a small voice.

"If I can."

"Caldwell has control over Margaret's mind. Will…will she go back to normal when she gets away from him?"

The pleading look in her eyes tore at him. "I got back to normal," he said, almost choking on the words, since in the eyes of the world "normal" hardly described him. He also didn't bother to say that he didn't know anyone else who had escaped from the Master's clutches.

"We can talk more later," he said. "I have a job to do in Baltimore tonight. Another 'eviction.'"

She looked so disappointed, he almost couldn't bear it.

"Eat," he said. "Get your strength back. You can read any of the books in the library. Or watch TV. I have satellite. I'll be back before morning."

"Okay," she said in a low voice.

Turning away from her reproachful look, he walked to the front hall. He grabbed a Stetson off the hat rack and turned to leave. Then he stopped and began retracing his steps, locking the door to his office on his way to the basement. He locked that door behind him as well.

In his bedroom, he showered and donned black jeans, a black T-shirt and black boots. He added a black leather jacket and brought along the Stetson.

TRAILBLAZER WATCHED the sleek little Acura sports coupe come down the road. Vickers was behind the wheel. Which meant this could be the perfect time to slip into the house and do some snooping. Of course, the surveillance system would pick him up. But with the master of the house otherwise occupied, that might not matter.

He sat on his motorcycle hidden in the woods, debating his options, then decided to follow Vickers and see what he was up to now.

He pulled out of the woods and followed a secondary road to the highway, where he picked up the Acura again. Too bad he hadn't been able to put a transponder on it. But Vickers's hidden garage was locked up tighter than the Pentagon.

Dropping back, he almost lost Vickers, then spotted him turning onto the Baltimore Beltway.

When it became clear where the man was heading, Trailblazer reached for his cell phone.

NICK STRUGGLED to keep his mind on business. As he'd told Emma, his current job was similar to the one he'd done for the Dayton Acres folks. Except that the problems in Baltimore were somewhat more serious than out in Howard County. A neighborhood association, frustrated that their section of the city was going downhill fast, wanted him to clear the crackheads out of an abandoned house in their midst.

To avoid attracting attention, he stayed below the speed limit. For a moment he considered the irony of that. He'd been born on an estate in Kent, not far from Canterbury, in England, well before the automobile was invented. Back in those days, one would have spent an entire day getting from Howard County to Baltimore. Now he could make the trip in under a half hour.

He'd visited nearly all the cities of the world, but he still preferred the countryside, which seemed to be disappearing at a fairly rapid rate on the east coast of the United States.

He wondered how long he could stay in his old Victorian. With housing developments proliferating in Howard County, a man who slept all day and came out only at night was bound to raise questions sooner or later. And then Nicholas Vickers would have to disappear. He'd have to take up a new identity—again. But not yet. Not until he finished his business around here.

And that included Damien Caldwell. The

trouble was, he hadn't counted on Emma Birmingham pushing him to act before he was ready.

NICK DROVE SLOWLY past the crack house. It was on a residential street lined with narrow Baltimore row houses, some still faced with the original brick but others sporting Formstone—a modern abomination that looked to be concocted of colored cement and mica and scored to resemble real cut stone.

Some of the properties were well kept. Others had definitely seen better days. And he felt sorry for the upstanding residents whose neighborhood was slowly being taken over by low-life creeps.

The vacant house where the druggies congregated or flopped was two doors in from a corner, making it convenient for the drifters to evacuate if and when the police came by—which evidently wasn't very often. Then, when the coast was clear, the low-lifes simply oozed back a couple of days later.

Nick had gotten the lay of the land during his preliminary surveillance of the place when the neighborhood association had first contacted him. Now he watched a man with filthy hair and a tattered coat climb the marble steps to the front door. Marble steps—a Baltimore tradition left over from a bygone era.

Recognizing the intractability of the gang and

drug problems the neighborhood was facing, he'd come prepared to inflict some damage. Actually, he was looking forward to it. He'd worked up quite a bit of tension in his dealings with Emma Birmingham, and now this job would give him the chance to cut loose.

Wondering how many people were inside, Nick turned the corner and found a parking space about halfway down the block. He retrieved the currently fashionable cowboy hat from the back seat and set it on his head, tipping the brim so that it hid his face.

Then he walked up the alley that approached the property from the rear. He waited in the deep shadows for a half hour, watching men and women meander in and out of the trash-littered backyard.

Two men sitting on a faded sofa got up and ambled away. Another guy flopped back against the sprung cushions and stared into space.

Nick held back. Something felt wrong about the scene. Something he couldn't put his finger on. So he waited another twenty minutes.

Finally he decided that the unsettled feeling in his gut came from the conversation he'd had with Emma before he left the house.

He'd come here to do a job and get some much-needed distance from Emma. So he'd better get down to business.

When he saw yet another stoner stagger out of the house, Nick acted. Maybe because he was still wound up over Emma, his assault was stronger than it should have been. He picked up the guy, dragged him unceremoniously into some scraggly bushes and bent his head back.

The guy struggled, but Nick sent him a brain zap that turned his arm and leg muscles to jelly. All the guy could do was stare wide-eyed up at his captor. His lips moved as he tried to form words, but only a whiny, panicked sound emerged.

Nick held the man in his rigid grasp, sinking his fangs into the flesh of his neck, and began to draw blood. But he didn't take much; it was rank with whatever drug the guy had pumped into his system.

With a feeling of disgust, Nick pulled back, hoping he wouldn't get buzzed from the joy juice circulating in the guy's system. He gazed down at the red drops glistening on the man's neck and knew he should seal the small wounds he'd made. But the idea of putting his mouth on the guy again turned his stomach.

Instead, he sent the man a jolt of mindless terror and watched him stagger away as fast as he could.

After wiping his mouth on the sleeve of his jacket, Nick decided it was time to clean out the rest of the druggies. He started toward the house. But someone inside must have seen him. He was only halfway across the yard when the shooting started.

## Chapter Eight

Nick felt a bullet whiz past his head and realized it had gone right through the crown of his hat.

Instinctively, he ducked, but the evasive action was too late. With the next shot he felt hot steel slam into his shoulder.

Whoever was shooting from inside the house must have seen him take the hit, because he heard a whoop of satisfaction.

"I got the narc! Did you see that? I got the bastard. Let's go out and finish him off."

"Stay back, man!" another voice shouted.

A barrage of bullets buzzed like angry wasps around him. Another slug sliced through his flesh, this time plowing into his chest, and he gasped from the sudden hot pain.

If he were human, Nick was pretty sure he would soon be dead. Instead, he fought to endure the agony no mere human could have sustained.

This was like the time in France when he'd helped save Caldwell's castle from attack.

But then he'd been mortal. Not now. Still, his whole left side and his chest were on fire and at the same time felt encased in cement. He knew hot blood was trickling down the inside of his shirt.

He hadn't come here intending to kill anyone, but self-defense was another matter. Crouching behind the now vacant sofa, he pulled out the gun he'd brought just in case. Teeth gritted, he returned fire simply to inform the bastards inside that he was still in the game.

He had the satisfaction of hearing a scream from inside the house. He'd gotten one of them.

At that moment, bright lights hit him in the face, and he could hear shrill babbling in the background.

Good Lord, now what? It sounded as if some media type was excitedly reporting breaking news.

With one arm up to block the blinding glare, he saw a television cameraman, along with the intrepid reporter, creeping toward him. He blinked rapidly in disbelief. Both men were apparently too stupid to live. Well, let them die if they wanted to. Nick was getting the hell out of there.

NO BOOK WAS GOING to hold her interest at the moment, Emma decided after browsing through

Nick's library. Television took less effort, so she turned on the set in what looked like a den and flipped through the channels.

On TLC, two middle-American couples had swapped homes, and one was painting the other's dining room a burnt orange. On TMC she saw yet another rerun of *Casablanca*. Finally, a local access channel caught her attention. She thought she was watching some kind of low-budget cop show, but after twenty seconds or so she realized it was a live report. A news team covering an inner-city Baltimore church's neighborhood improvement efforts had heard that a shoot-out was taking place a couple of blocks away.

They'd hustled over to the scene, and now a news-man in a rumpled pin-striped suit was babbling excitedly, giving a play-by-play account of a gunfight between the residents of a crack house and someone outside.

As the camera angle swung to the left, she caught her breath. The man now on the screen was wearing a leather jacket and a Stetson just like the one Nick had grabbed from the hall rack before he'd headed downstairs to get ready for his current job.

She wanted it to be a coincidence. But, oh God—no. It *was* Nick. She couldn't see his eyes, but she recognized his nose and his lips. He staggered back, and it looked as if he'd been hit.

He hauled himself out of the frame, and the camera tried to follow him, but he disappeared down a dark alley, moving way too rapidly for a man with a bullet in his body.

CROUCHING LOW and hoping his hat completely hid his face, Nick executed a strategic retreat from both the gunfire and the camera. The buzzing in his ears made it difficult for him to think. He figured it was the roaring of his own blood in his head. Then he realized he was hearing sirens. Ambulances and police cars.

Finally, the cops were on their way—trailing the news guys by almost twenty minutes.

What a city!

He made it, undiscovered, to the end of the alley, then had to stop because his head was spinning and his breath was coming in great gasps.

He'd lost a lot of blood. Too much. The need for sustenance clawed at his insides. And he was prepared to grab the first victim he encountered. But he was alone in the alley.

He feared he was too weak to stagger any farther. Then he saw a cop car turn the corner at the end of the block.

He could have handled one officer and sunk his fangs into the guy's neck. But in his weakened condition, he couldn't take on two armed cops.

Hoping he hadn't been spotted yet, he pressed himself against a high wooden fence at the back of a house. It helped hold him up, but he lost his hat in the process. Too weary to bend down and pick it up, he forced himself to move on, sliding his body along the vertical surface. When he came to a gate, his heart gave a lurch of hope. He fumbled with the rusted latch, it gave way, and he fell into someone's backyard.

He wanted to simply lie there on the small patio, but the cool bricks revived him a little, and he knew that the open gate would be a dead giveaway of his location. So he shoved himself up and eased the gate closed behind him.

He stared up at the back of the house before him. It was completely dark. He hoped that meant no one was home. Careful not to bump into any garden furniture or planters, he headed for the basement door under a small cement porch. He tugged open the warped door and stumbled down the steps to an unfinished storage area, where he lowered himself to the cement floor, propping his back against a wall. When his head thudded softly against the wall, he heard a hollow sound. Was there a space behind the wall where he could hide? Maybe, but at the moment, he didn't have the energy to investigate.

He was still in agonizing pain, but he knew his body had the power to heal his wounds if he could only feed. Rolling to his back, he stared up at the steps and considered that if he'd been shot dead center to the heart, that could have killed even him. So he'd probably sustained a bullet to a lung.

His vampire constitution would take care of that, but not unless he replenished his blood supply soon. And then there was the sun to worry about.

His body bathed in perspiration and pain, he tried to make plans. Morning would come in a few hours. Then what? Perhaps he should hope for a cloudy day. That would help, but not enough.

From his hiding place in the darkness, he cast his mind outward, searching for help. But he was too weak to summon anyone to himself.

Except Jeanette. She would come to him.

Jeanette? Was that right? Was he waiting for Jeanette?

EMMA FELT UTTER TERROR clutch her throat. A few days ago, the only thing she'd known about Nicholas Vickers was that he was a private investigator and that Damien Caldwell considered him a dangerous enemy.

So she'd come to his house to convince him to help her rescue Margaret. Then she'd gotten shot—and he'd cured her in some mysterious way that she still didn't understand.

Tonight it looked as if *he'd* been shot, and she felt a gut-wrenching fear for his life.

"Nick," she whispered, her gaze riveted to the television screen. "Oh Lord, Nick."

If he'd cured her, could he do the same thing to himself?

On the television, sirens sounded. Then the live feed focused on a couple of police cruisers and an ambulance arriving. Uniformed cops jumped out and ran toward the camera, and the picture jerked as they pushed the news team back and out of the way.

"The police have just closed off the area," the reporter said. "Officer, can you tell us what's going on?"

"Get out of the way," the cop snarled. "Before you get shot."

The picture swung wildly, and the commentary stopped abruptly.

Finally, the camera again focused on the reporter. In the background, Emma could see news vans from other stations arriving and reporters jumping out.

"We will continue to give you information as we get it!" the man she'd been listening to shouted as the police pushed him farther back.

"Yeah, I'll bet," Emma muttered. "If they don't arrest you for near fatal stupidity."

Now that the reporter and his cameraman had been shoved away from the action, the picture on the screen shifted to the crowd that had gathered on the street corner, and Emma turned away, knowing she wasn't going to learn anything more substantive until the cops released some information.

Which might not be until morning, for all she knew.

Fighting the tightness in her throat, she paced back and forth across the Oriental rug. She had only met Nick a few days ago, but she'd already felt connected to him in her dreams, and she ached to go to him now, to help him in any way she could.

He'd told her to stay put, rest and wait for him to come home. But she knew she couldn't simply sit here waiting for news, watching the drama unfold on television.

Dashing up to the room where she'd been staying, she grabbed her purse. By the time she'd run downstairs again, she knew she had another problem. She didn't have a key to the house. If she left, she couldn't just leave the doors unlocked. What if those awful bikers came back? And she had no idea how to set the security alarm.

Angry with Nick for leaving her in this fix and angry with herself for not thinking to at least ask for a key, she paced into the kitchen. Wait. Didn't everyone have a catch-all drawer in the kitchen, crammed with miscellaneous items such as rubber bands, twist ties, bottle openers and keys?

Sure enough, even Nick's stage set of a kitchen had such a drawer, complete with several loose keys. She took them to the front door and tested them. When she found one that worked, she let out a sigh of relief and hurried to lock all the doors. If Nick's security system wasn't activated, locking up would have to do.

Stepping onto the front porch, she stopped short when a shadow emerged from the nearby woods. In the next second, she let out a nervous laugh. It was only a deer, grazing on a bush. It didn't even bother to run away when she stepped off the porch.

She'd left her car in the driveway, and panic gripped her when she saw that the spot was empty. She ordered herself to stay calm. Nick hadn't taken her rental back to the airport. He must have stashed it somewhere.

She began to search the grounds around the house, and twenty minutes later she found the car behind a stand of trees.

With a sigh of relief, she climbed in and headed for the city, unsure exactly what she'd do when she got there.

She did know the area of the shoot-out from the broadcast, and she stopped at a gas station to get directions to the general location. When she approached the inner-city neighborhood, she saw that the police had cordoned off the disreputable-looking house and the alley behind it. After finding a parking space nearby, she got out of the car and wormed her way to the front of the crowd of onlookers just as an ambulance was pulling away from the curb.

She turned to an especially eager-looking observer next to her. "I just got here. Who's in the ambulance?" she asked.

"A guy from the crack house. Got shot by some dude in the backyard."

"Anyone else hurt?" she tried to ask casually.

The man gave her a speculative look as he brushed his hair back from his forehead. "You a reporter? You want to interview me?"

She forced a laugh. "No. Just nosy."

"Well, the way I heard it, the dude outside got shot, too. But he got away, and the cops are lookin' for him."

"Hmm," she forced herself to reply indifferently even as her pulse pounded in alarm. Nick was injured and evading the authorities. Maybe that was all in a day's work for a private investigator, but it was more than her heart could take.

She slipped out of the crowd and headed down the block, then circled around toward the alley. But she could see a police car blocking her way.

Nick could be anywhere, she supposed, but if he'd been shot, she had to assume he couldn't have gotten very far. She circled the block, looking between row houses and, once she got farther away from the police car, called Nick's name.

She saw nothing. Heard nothing. And she wondered if she was wasting time here. Maybe Nick had made it back to his car and was on his way to a hospital—or, more likely, home. Maybe the best thing to do was go back to his house and wait for him. But she couldn't shake the nagging feeling that he needed her. And she had to find him.

She rounded the block again with no success, even peering under the bushes in the tiny front yards in case he had tried to hide in the greenery and was lying there, unconscious.

With a shudder, she drove that image from her mind. Something was drawing her back to that alley behind the crack house Nick had disappeared into. But was there any way she could get in there?

NICK TRIED TO PUSH himself up, but he didn't have the strength. He was in some dark, damp place. And he couldn't see very well, which was strange, because his night vision was excellent.

He was waiting for…Jeanette, he remembered. She was so sweet. And so smart, too. She had been educated in a convent, and the nuns had taught her well. But they had also guarded her like the precious jewel she was. In worldly ways she was utterly naive. He had been captivated with her at once.

He'd never been much interested in poetry, but she'd introduced him to the great poets. John Keats, Christopher Marlowe, George Herbert, Alexander Pope.

Shakespeare had become his favorite, and he'd memorized some of his sonnets to recite to her. He knew she'd be so pleased.

*Shall I compare thee to a summer's day?* he'd say.

*Thou art more lovely and more temperate* .

He smiled dreamily, anticipating her pleasure and surprise. He should get up and wash and comb his hair before she arrived. He reached out, felt a wooden panel and tried to push himself up. But the panel caved in.

Bloody hell. He'd broken the damn bed.

Or something.

EMMA APPROACHED the back alley. The cops there were looking the other way, which gave her a chance to peek down it. In the illumination from their headlights, she spotted an object on the ground.

A Stetson. Just like the one Nick had grabbed from the hall rack before going out. He'd still been wearing it when she'd seen the television picture of him fleeing the shooting scene.

She wanted to rush forward, but no way would she get past those cops.

Stumped, she withdrew a bit and sat down on a set of marble front steps. She'd come all this way to help Nick—only to run into a wall.

Frantically, her mind scrambled for a plan. What was she going to do—start knocking on doors and asking if she could go into the backyard and look for a man who'd been shot? Yeah, sure. Then she thought about one of the many cities where she'd lived. Mom had been between marriages, and she'd rented a town house in an older neighborhood. Between their house and the next had been a passageway leading to their backyard. Jumping up, she started down the row of houses again, concentrating on the junctions where each house was connected to the next, looking for something similar.

In the darkness she found one. She wanted to pull out the penlight she carried in her purse, but didn't want to call attention to herself if anyone was watching. Instead, she stepped into the passage, holding her hands in front of her and walking cautiously toward the patch of gray at the other end.

When she reached it, she heard voices and froze. Someone was in the backyard. The cops?

Then a woman giggled, and a man's laughter joined in. Apparently she'd been about to interrupt two people relaxing in their backyard.

Silently withdrawing, she headed farther down the block, seeking the next passageway.

HUDDLED IN THE DARKNESS, Nick felt cold seeping into his bones. He didn't have much time left. He knew he should try to hang on to consciousness, but right now his dreams were better.

Jeanette was with him, smiling at him, raising her lips to his. He bent to kiss her, marveling that she had come back to him after all these years.

"My sweet," he murmured. "At last."

A cold chill traveled over his skin as he dimly realized he couldn't be with Jeanette. She was in heaven. And if he died, he would go straight to the flames of hell, where he belonged.

He licked his dry lips. He had lived for over a hundred and fifty years. He thought of his childhood. Of his tutors. Of riding across the fields on a fast steed. Of sneaking down to the river to swim with his beloved brothers even though their father had expressly forbidden them to risk its dangerous currents.

He remembered a deliciously hot summer in southern Italy when he'd been sixteen and lost his virginity. He thought about his first hot-air balloon ride. And his first biplane.

He had always craved danger and excitement. And he had already lived more years than any man had a right to claim. But he didn't want it to end under a stairwell in a dark, dank basement.

MOVING DOWN the row of houses, Emma found another passageway, just as dark and just as forbidding as the first one.

But she plunged in, moving more quickly this time.

When she emerged from the passage, she was standing on a brick patio dotted with lawn furniture and planters. Rose bushes. Columbine. Day lilies. A clematis climbing a pole near the back door of the house.

Fighting the tightness in her chest, she called Nick's name.

When he didn't answer, she turned to leave. She'd just stepped back into the little alley when she heard a groan. Nick!

But then she heard voices at the other end of the alleyway. The cops! They were coming closer, apparently checking the backyards.

Oh, Lord, were they about to find Nick's hiding place? She turned and took a step back toward the house, and she heard his voice drift up to her like a whisper carried on a spring breeze.

"Jeanette!"

Jeanette. The name of his lost love. Was he so badly hurt that he was hallucinating? Where was he?

"Nick!" Desperately, she scanned the area and she spotted a door ajar under the back stairs. It must lead to a basement. She hurried to it.

"Nick, are you down there?" she whispered urgently.

"'When in disgrace with fortune and men's eyes...'" she heard him say softly. He was there!

It took her a moment to recognize he'd recited the first line of a Shakespearean sonnet, one her tenth-grade English teacher had made the class memorize.

"Nick? Answer me," she called softly into the darkness, trying to make her way down the unlit steps. Behind her she heard the gate at the back of the patio rattle.

Damn! The cops.

Frantically, she turned back to close the warped door behind her and stumbled down the dark stairs, one hand against the wall to guide her.

## Chapter Nine

Nick fought to clear the fog from his brain. There was Emma Birmingham, standing at the bottom of the steps.

Emma. Not Jeanette. They weren't in nineteenth-century France. They were in twenty-first-century Baltimore. In a tight spot.

The cops were after him. And her, too—unless he did something about it.

He tried to sit up, and he heard her gasp.

"Nick? Is that you?" she whispered.

"Yeah. Reach out for me." She stretched out her arm, and he caught her hand. Then, with what little strength he had left, he pushed at the panel behind him. It wasn't part of a bed, as he'd thought in his dream. It was some kind of storage compartment. Big enough for two people, he hoped.

"Nick, what are you doing? The cops are coming!" she whispered urgently.

"Get down on your hands and knees. Hurry. Come with me!" he whispered.

Without hesitation, she dropped to all fours and followed him through the darkness into a tightly enclosed space.

As he attempted to slide the wooden panel back into place behind them, he couldn't hold back a low groan of pain.

"Oh, Nick, is it bad?"

"Hush," he whispered, "or they'll find us."

EMMA ACHED to examine his wound. But she clamped her lips together, obeying his orders.

She remained still in the darkness, hearing heavy footsteps from the patio above them. Beside her, she felt waves of tension radiating from Nick's body.

Through a narrow gap around the panel behind which they were hiding, she saw the beam of a flashlight knifing into the stairwell and swinging around, inspecting the area. Her breath stilled as she waited for footsteps to come down the steps.

Sure enough, one of the cops came partway down, and the light grew more intense.

She waited for him to come all the way down, pull the barrier aside and expose them to his flashlight beam.

He stayed where he was.

Then he turned and went back up the steps.

"See anything?" his partner asked.

"Nah. Just some tools."

"Let's try the next yard."

The footsteps receded. But Emma didn't let out the breath she'd been holding until she heard the gate hinges squeak again.

Beside her, Nick slumped against the wall.

Fumbling in the darkness, she found his hand and clutched his fingers. "How bad off are you?" she asked.

"I'm fine."

"I don't think so." With her free hand she fumbled for her penlight and turned it on to inspect him.

He made a groaning sound. "Don't!"

"Sorry." She quickly aimed the beam away from him and at the wooden panel they were closeted behind.

"The Compte de St. Germaine is going to be livid," he said.

"What?"

"You were under his protection."

"Do you mean that *Jeanette* was under someone's protection?" she asked carefully.

"You know your father paid him to find a suitable husband for you."

His mind was obviously in another time and place. She pressed her fingers to his forehead, expecting to find him burning up. Instead, he was cold as ice.

"I think you're in shock. How bad is your wound?"

He cleared his throat. "What makes you think I'm wounded?"

"I saw the shoot-out on television. And an onlooker said you'd been hit."

"Television? Bloody hell!"

She tipped her head to one side. "Where did you get that curse from, anyway?"

He laughed, but the laugh turned into a groan. Still, he managed to say, "I read historical novels. One of my hobbies, you know."

"Like reading Shakespeare."

"Yeah."

"Do you… Do you know who I am?" she asked carefully.

"Of course. You're Emma. Emma Birmingham."

"Yes. But a little while ago you thought I was someone else." She tried to read his expression but in the dim light was unable to. "Let's take a look at your wound."

She reached for the front of his jacket, but he caught her wrist before she could make contact with the dark leather. "No!" he barked.

"Nick, you're hurt. We have to tend to that," she pointed out.

He raised a hand to stroke her hair. He was trembling, but he leaned forward to nuzzle her neck.

"Nick?"

"I'm sorry," he said in a gritty voice.

"Sorry about what?" she asked. But then she forgot the question. Her limbs felt oddly heavy, and her mind was suddenly muzzy. Why was it so difficult to manage a coherent thought?

"What's…happening to me?" she asked, hearing her own voice sound faint and far away.

"You're still recovering from getting hurt the other day. You're exhausted. You need to sleep."

"No. I need to help…you."

"You will. You're the only one who can."

She wanted to ask him what he meant, but the thought simply drifted away, and she leaned forward, her head falling against Nick's shoulder.

"I'm sorry."

Hadn't he said that before? "About what?" she asked blearily.

"Taking advantage of you."

He skimmed his lips over her cheek, her eyebrow. At the same time, his hand moved downward, stroking her neck, her shoulder, the top of one breast.

She felt peaceful yet aroused. "Are you…going to make love with me?"

He chuckled softly.

Had they done that before? They had done something in his bed. But she couldn't exactly remember what, not when her mind was full of cotton candy.

He tipped her head back and pressed his lips to her neck again, and she felt a jolt of fear. His teeth... What was he doing with his teeth?

"Nick...don't." She tried to struggle, but he held her fast.

"Emma, please..."

"No. Stop." Her alarm gave way to a deep sense of calm. Then intense pleasure. And then she was simply drifting on a wave of arousal....

AT THE REFUGE, Damien Caldwell switched off the television. It was clear that the reporters were reduced to repeating the same bits of information over and over.

At least he knew the basics. Someone had tried to sneak up on a crack house in Baltimore and whoever it was had gotten into a shoot-out with the people inside.

He was pretty sure who was involved. The basic setup looked like the handiwork of Nicholas Vickers, "private investigator." The vampire crusader. The guy who thought he was better than Damien Caldwell because he came from a rich and privileged background, while Damien was the son of a camel driver who had sold him into slavery.

He snorted. Two years ago Mr. Vickers had set up shop out in Howard County. Since then the so-called private detective had become a one-man vigilante-justice service.

Damien had been keeping track of him for quite some time. Before the bastard had come to the Baltimore area, he'd been out in San Francisco for a while, until he got into some trouble with the police.

After that he'd changed his name and resurfaced in Maryland. Damien knew it was no coincidence that Vickers was living within seventy-five miles of his own pleasant enclave on the Miles River. Close, but not too close.

Sooner or later, Vickers would come after him. And he wanted to be ready. So he welcomed any chance he got to acquire more information. The television news report was certainly a piece of luck.

Damien laughed, then leaned back in his chair and laced his fingers together across his middle.

The modern age was beyond anything he could have imagined. He'd wanted to check up on Nicholas Vickers—and there he was on television. Too bad for Vickers that he couldn't just stay in his carefully secured Victorian home and mind his own business. It appeared he'd been wounded. With any luck the bastard would bleed to death, and leave him alone for good.

WITH NO FINESSE and a feeling that bordered on desperation, Nick sank his fangs into Emma's neck. He feared he barely had control of her mind. But he had to satisfy his terrible craving for blood—a thirst more horrible than he ever could have imagined. He was so depleted that his veins and arteries were near collapsing, the tissues of his body turning dry as chalk.

But as her blood flowed into his mouth, he felt his sense of control return.

He had been so greedy for sustenance that he barely cared what woman he held in his arms. She could have been Sandy, the blonde from the bar. But as his senses came back, so did his appreciation of Emma Birmingham. Her scent. The feel of her pliant body in his arms. The soft roundness of her breasts as he caressed them. And the sense of connection with her. It had started with the dreams. Then she had come looking for him, asking for his help. But she was in Baltimore tonight because she'd wanted to help *him*.

He was profoundly grateful for that. No, beyond grateful. He felt so much more—emotions he barely dared to acknowledge.

He ached to give her pleasure, to pay her back for his life with at least that much. But he knew there was no time for that now.

They both had to get out of here before the cops came back. So he took only enough blood to give him the strength to stand and walk and to defend them both if need be.

When he pulled his fangs from her flesh, she

made a sound of protest. "Come back to me," she whispered.

"No. That's enough." His tongue stroked over her skin to seal the wounds, then he laid her on her back.

"What are you doing?"

"Just sleep. You need to rest."

Nick stroked back a lock of Emma's silky hair, sending her calming thoughts, even when his own emotions were in turmoil.

Her eyes fluttered closed, and she relaxed into sleep. She needed that after the bloodletting. But he couldn't give her much time. Only a few minutes. As he watched her, his stomach muscles clenched. Drinking from her had been his only option. He'd done it quickly, trying to focus on something besides the pleasure of it.

But it had been pleasure, even in his weakened state.

And now she was the weak one, because this was the second time in two days he had drawn from her. That was too much. But he had had no choice. She had come to him when he was hovering near death, and he had taken what she offered.

Not that she had offered her blood freely, of course. But she *had* wanted to save him, just as she had when she'd come charging down his cellar stairs hours before. Both times, he acknowledged, he had taken advantage of her compassion.

"Bloody hell," he muttered again.

He was still way below his usual strength, but he had enough blood to function until he got home and could visit his deer herd.

Easing away from Emma, he struggled out of his jacket and then his shirt. The leather showed obvious bullet holes, and the T-shirt was soaked with blood.

He looked down, trying to inspect the wounds, but because of the angle he couldn't really see them without a mirror. Lucky for him that the myth about a vampire's not having a reflection was bunk. Instead, he ran his hands over the entry points. Though he had bled profusely, now that he had taken sustenance, the wounds were already healing. Soon all evidence of his near-fatal encounter would vanish entirely.

Satisfied, he pulled the jacket back on and zipped it. He wanted to get rid of the bloody shirt so Emma wouldn't see it, but leaving it here would be a bad move. If the police returned and found this cubbyhole, they would have DNA to analyze—and they would come up with some pretty strange conclusions.

So he stuffed the shirt into his pocket, then looked down at Emma. Her eyes were closed, and her breathing was deep and even. He hated to disturb her, but they had to get out of here.

"Emma?" He stroked her cheek, then leaned down to replace his fingers with his lips.

Her eyelids fluttered open. "Would you recite some more poetry to me?" she asked dreamily.

"When we get home."

"You're a very sensitive man," she said softly.

He snorted, and abruptly she looked confused, as if she was trying to make sense of what was going on. "What happened? Did I faint or something?"

"Yes. I told you you needed to rest."

"How could I rest? You were in danger. *We* were in danger," she added as her mind cleared. "We still are!"

"We bought ourselves some time," he answered, hoping it was true. "Where did you leave your car?"

She thought for a moment. "Around the corner from the crack house."

Her vehicle was closer. "Okay. We'll take your car."

"What do we do about yours?"

"I'll get it later."

She pushed herself up and looked toward the hole in the wall where he'd removed the wooden panel. "In this neighborhood, you'll probably come back to find it stripped."

"I'll take my chances," he answered, not worried about a mere automobile. Investments over the years had made him rich, even by modern standards. "Let's go, before the cops come back."

He eased himself out of the cubbyhole and stood, then bent to offer her his hand. She climbed out and stood, too, then swayed on her feet. "I'm dizzy," she said in a puzzled voice.

"Like I said, you should be in bed resting."

"Hah! Lucky for you I was up watching television."

"Yes. Very lucky." He hugged her to him, feeling the knot of guilt in his stomach twist painfully. He'd taken too much blood from her in too short a time.

"I'm okay now," she said, straightening up. "Let's go."

"We'll take it slow."

But she remained still, staring at the front of his jacket; she'd spotted one of the bullet holes. "You said you weren't hurt!"

"I wasn't. My jacket was unzipped and hanging open, " he improvised. "A bullet must have gone through it."

"I don't believe you. I know you were hurt. Let me see." She unzipped the jacket and bared his naked chest. "Where's your shirt?"

"I didn't wear one," he lied.

She ran her fingers over his flesh and found the indentation of his rapidly healing bullet wound.

"What's this?"

"An old scar," he lied again, glad that the darkness prevented her from taking a closer look. "Come on. We have to get out of here."

Now that they were out of the hole in the ground, he could see how close it was to dawn. Not good. Still, he kept his voice even. "But once we get out of the backyard, it's better if we don't look like we're in a tearing hurry."

They climbed the steps and reached the small patio, and he started toward the back gate.

"Wait. There are two cops at the end of the alley."

With his renewed blood supply, he knew he could easily handle the pair, but he couldn't let Emma see him do that.

"We don't have to go that way," she said. "I got in here from the street. There's a passageway to the front of the house."

She led him to it, and they emerged on the sidewalk.

He could see that even that small exertion had left her winded. "Take it easy," he said, steadying her against his side.

"I'm…I'm fine."

"Which way is your car?"

Turning, she started up the block, still leaning against him.

He was starting to think they had gotten away clean. But when they had made it past half a dozen houses, a uniformed officer came out the front door and down the stairs of the seventh one.

"Bloody hell," Nick muttered.

Emma tensed. "What?"

"A cop." Nick knew he could have gotten away by sprinting in the other direction, but that wasn't an option right now—not when he was holding Emma up.

The officer reached the sidewalk and fixed his gaze on them, eyeing Nick's leather jacket. Nick was profoundly glad that Emma's body hid the bullet holes.

"Good evening, officer," he said politely.

"Kinda late for a stroll, especially around here, don't you think?" the cop asked suspiciously.

"We heard about all the excitement down here earlier, and we thought we'd have a look-see," Nick answered. "But the whole area was blocked off."

The officer, whose nametag identified him as Murphy, said, "You don't want to go rushing to a crime scene, you know. You could get hurt."

"Yeah, I suppose you're right," Nick agreed.

Murphy stayed firmly in their path. Probably he'd had a frustrating night of knocking on doors and getting unhelpful responses.

"You two sure you didn't see anything?" the

cop pressed, maybe hoping he had a couple of potential witnesses on hand.

"Not a thing," Nick replied.

The officer turned to Emma, fixing her with a stern look. "What about you? See anybody leaving the area in a hurry? A tall guy on foot? Maybe wounded?"

"No, sir."

The officer gave them another long look, lingering on Nick's leather jacket, and he tensed. The cop had probably gotten a description of the elusive gunman—including his attire. But since Emma was still leaning against him like a woman in love, the officer couldn't make the puzzle pieces fit together.

Murphy gave them both one more long look, then reached into his breast pocket and produced a business card. "You see anything, you remember anything, you give me a call."

"Sure thing," Nick answered.

As the cop started for the next house on the block, Nick let out a small sigh—and felt Emma sag against him.

"He suspected something," she whispered.

"You think?" he said glibly. He held Emma tightly to his side as they made their way to her car.

He wanted to hurry her along, but he knew she was exhausted from her recent bloodletting.

After what felt like a century, they finally

reached her car. She fumbled in the purse still slung over her shoulder and brought out the keys to the rental.

Deftly, he lifted them out of her hand. "I'll drive."

Once she was belted into the passenger seat, he started for home. He wanted to floor it but knew that was a bad idea. So he gritted his teeth and stayed just above the speed limit.

Beside him, Emma dozed, then woke with a start. "Where are we?"

"On the way to my place."

"Are you going to tell me what exactly happened back at that crack house?"

"I was doing surveillance to determine how best to approach the job I'd been hired to do. Someone inside shot at me. I returned fire to get whoever it was to back off."

"And hit him?"

He made a dismissive sound. "If I did, I'd say that was pure luck. I couldn't see a thing."

"He could be dead," she said in a fretful voice.

He wanted to say it would serve the bastard right. Instead, he pressed his lips together, reached for the radio dial, and tuned in to an all-news station; undoubtedly it would be updating the local story with endless, breathless, pointless, speculative "commentary." After a string of commercials, the reporter did, in fact, return to the shoot-out.

"One occupant of the house was taken to Union Memorial Hospital and is in stable condition. The gunman from outside the house is still at large. He is described as a white male, six feet tall, wearing a black leather jacket, a black Stetson and black jeans. He may have been wounded."

"That's a pretty good description," he muttered.

"Except you lost the hat. You'd think they would have spotted it by now. I did," she said.

He swung his gaze toward her. "Are you going to turn me in?" he asked.

"Of course not!"

"What if the guy had died?"

He could see her considering her answer.

"Well, if it was self-defense…"

"It was."

He was silent for several moments, thinking. He owed Emma his life—and his liberty. He should be offering her something in return. But he knew what she would ask for, so he kept silent.

As if she were following his thoughts, she said, "Take me to Caldwell's compound."

His hands clenched on the wheel. "You don't know what you're saying. You can't just go rushing back into the Refuge."

"My sister is there. I have to get her out."

"You already tried, didn't you?"

She made an angry sound. "Yes! And she

wouldn't go. But you could carry her out of there."

He wanted to explain to her all the reasons why rushing in would be a dangerous mistake. "I told you to let me think about it," he said.

"Well, don't take too long."

His head whipped toward her. "Is that a threat?"

## Chapter Ten

Nick waited for Emma's answer.

"Take it any way you like," she muttered, folding her arms across her chest.

Thankful that they were almost home, he turned onto his tree-shaded lane. He had felt sunlight begin seeping through the windows of the car, digging into his skin, biting his nerve endings like the teeth of a small, gnawing animal. If he didn't get inside soon, he would start to burn.

He dragged in a grateful breath when he pulled into his driveway and activated the secret garage door.

Emma's eyes widened when she saw the retaining wall open.

"That's a fake wall?"

"Yeah." He drove into the blessed darkness and cut the engine. If Emma hadn't been there, he would have sat behind the wheel for several minutes, drinking in the cool dimness soothing his skin.

But he had more urgent business than his own singed hide. He had to help Emma regain her strength. Exiting the car, he strode to a switch beside the garage door and turned on a low-watt light. Not that he needed the illumination, but Emma would. And the contractor certainly would have wondered about him if he'd refused to let him install it.

Emma climbed wearily out of the car and shut the passenger door. She flexed her arm, then reached to touch her side.

"You need more rest—and more treatment," Nick said.

"I'm fine," she protested.

"Obviously you're not. I'll give you something to help build you up."

She tipped her head to one side. "What—a tonic? Like one of our stepfathers used to give me?"

"Something like that."

She wrinkled her nose. "His tonic tasted like stagnant water."

"Mine tastes like fine wine."

"A likely story."

"I'll let you judge for yourself."

He led her through the tunnel into his private living quarters. From the linen closet he took out an oldfashioned green glass bottle containing a concoction mixed long ago by an herbalist in New Orleans; it was designed to build up the blood. He'd gotten it when he was involved with a woman named Theresa Emerson. He'd wanted to keep making love with her. And for a time, the tonic had kept her healthy. But only for a time.

He felt a pang when he remembered that episode in his life. He'd thought he could love Theresa, and giving her up had created an ache deep inside him.

The herbal elixir had prolonged their time together. But he'd known that the affair would have to end. If it didn't, he'd ultimately take too much of her blood. Doing without it when he was emotionally involved with a partner was like having intercourse with her over and over and never reaching climax. He'd known his self-control would ultimately crack, rendering his attraction to Theresa a fatal one. Fatal to her.

He poured a quarter cup of the burgundy-colored liquid into a crystal wineglass and handed it to Emma.

She took a cautious whiff, then a sip. "It's not too bad."

"Be honest. It's good."

"Okay. It's good."

"Drink up."

"Why don't you join me?"

"Because I don't need any. My blood's fine," he said, struggling to keep his voice even.

She did as he asked, then put the glass down.

"You'll take some more tonight."

"Is that an order?"

"It's a strong suggestion." He gave her a look. "Now, both of us have had a long, long night. We should get some sleep."

"Yes," she agreed, looking nearly asleep on her feet already.

She started for his bedroom, and he felt his heart clench inside his chest. He opened his mouth to say that she should go upstairs. But he simply couldn't make the words come out. And, he rationalized, if she was in his bed, at least he could keep an eye on her.

When he'd first become a vampire, he'd slept through the day as though he were dead. Then he'd trained himself to wake up and stay up for short periods. Now he could awaken readily during the day if he needed to.

His mouth turned dry as he watched Emma pull off her slacks and drape them over the back of a chair.

"I'm going to shower. I smell like I've been hiding in a hole in the ground," she murmured.

"Yes." He thought about joining her but decided that was a bad idea.

"May I borrow a T-shirt?"

"Sure," he said, his mouth dry. "What's your preference? Batman or plain black?"

"You have a thing for Batman?"

"I like his style." He handed her the superhero shirt, then made himself scarce in his game room while she showered. But when he tried to play "Dragon Combat," he was too uncoordinated to score. With a muttered curse, he conceded defeat to the opponent he'd picked up online, then withdrew from the game. But he stayed in the room, his ears tuned toward his houseguest.

He waited until Emma had climbed into bed, then took a quick shower and pulled on a clean T-shirt and undershorts. He would have liked to sleep in absolute darkness, but because she was with him, he left the bathroom light on and closed the door most of the way before slipping in beside her.

Her body heat radiated toward him, and it required effort to keep from gathering her into his arms.

Then she spoke—and increased his tension a hundredfold.

"Can we talk about the Refuge?"

He knew then that he'd made a mistake in more ways than one by allowing her into his bed. He sighed. "When we wake up."

She huffed out a breath but didn't argue. Which was good, because he was too worn out for sparring.

"We've both had a tough night," he pointed out. "We need to sleep. If you want to get something to eat later on, I left the alarm system off."

"Thanks."

He closed his eyes and felt unconsciousness take him.

Some time later he woke up, knowing instantly that something was wrong.

Light spilled from the bathroom into his eyes. His undershirt was rolled up around his armpits, and delicate fingers danced across his bare flesh.

He was disoriented, but he reacted instantly. His hand shot out, catching a small, feminine wrist.

Emma gasped.

"Bloody hell!"

When she tried to pull her hand away, he held her fast. "What are you doing?" he growled.

She gulped. "I woke up from a dream where you'd been shot. I was scared, and…and I had to look at your chest…to make sure you were okay."

"I'm fine."

She took her lower lip between her teeth, then released it. "You said you had old scars on your chest. Before, when I opened your jacket, I felt them. Now they're gone."

Feeling trapped, he wanted to curse again. Last night he'd still had small indentations where the bullets had entered his body. When he glanced down at his chest now, he saw that the marks were barely visible.

With a small shrug, he let go of her wrist. "I do have old scars there. I guess they looked different in the light of that cellar."

"I didn't *see* them. I *felt* them." She raised her face and looked at him. "What kind of game are you playing with me? What's going on?"

"Nothing!"

"You're lying." As she spoke, she climbed out of bed and marched toward the door.

He should simply let her go, he told himself. Out of the bedroom. Out of the house. Out of his life.

That would be the smart thing to do. But he had long since stopped being smart where Emma Birmingham was concerned. Now he well and truly understood why he'd allowed her to share his bed. He didn't just want to keep an eye on her. He wanted to make love with her. He wanted everything he had denied himself for too many long, lonely years.

His throat constricted. He couldn't have everything. He'd already taken blood from her twice. He couldn't do it again. Not so soon. But he *could* share with her what a mortal man might share....

Before she reached the door, he shot past her, blocking the exit.

She looked at him, blinking, obviously trying to figure out how he'd gotten there so fast.

"You…were just in bed," she said in a trembling voice.

"Uh-huh. And I didn't want to let you go."

As he folded her close, he heard himself utter a low sound that might have been a curse—or a plea. He didn't know which. Then he lowered his head so that his mouth could come down on hers.

Her lips were warm and soft yet somehow also challenging. The thought flashed through his mind that maybe she was asking for the honesty he had denied her.

He couldn't give her honesty. He couldn't give that to anyone. Never. And as he kissed her, he felt fear gather in his belly. Fear for her. Fear for himself as he experienced the intensity of his response to her.

He could cloud her mind, the way he always did when he made love to a mortal woman. But he didn't want to with Emma. And there was no need for that now, because he would take no more blood from her. He would make love with her, but he would deny himself the ultimate pleasure.

He knew she felt the waves of need coming off him. And maybe she was trying to prove to both of them that she wasn't afraid of him, because she moved in closer and angled her head so that he could kiss her more deeply.

He gladly accepted the invitation. Blood pounded in his ears as he tasted her again and again, deeply, roughly, then more gently as he heard her soft cries of pleasure. When he finally lifted his head, her body was plastered against his, and his palms were under her shirt, splayed against her back. They were both struggling for breath.

He reversed their positions, bracing his back against the door, opening his legs and bringing her hips into the cradle of his so that she could feel the erection straining at the front of his shorts.

When she made a small sound and moved against him, he felt his heart skip a beat.

She raised her face and looked into his eyes. "Nick, where are we going with this?" she whispered.

"Where do you want to go?"

"As far as you're willing to take me."

The words tore at him. He knew where he wanted to take her, but he couldn't go all the way. Not and live with himself.

"You should leave—while you still have the chance," he said honestly.

"Are you trying to scare me off?"

"Yes."

"Well, I'm staying right where I am."

"Oh, Lord, Emma." His hands were trembling

as they stroked her back. Then, with one smooth motion, he pulled the Batman T-shirt over her head, tossing it onto the floor.

She gasped as cool air hit her upper body.

He held her away from himself, his eyes roaming over her ivory skin, her breasts, the beautiful coral crests that were stiff and puckered for him. Reaching out, he cupped their fullness, his fingers stroking upward to glide across her perfect nipples.

He lifted his gaze to her face. Her skin was flushed a beautiful pink. She looked so exposed and vulnerable and at the same time so aroused that the sight of her took his breath away.

He could imagine his own face—dark and heated and vulnerable as well. In all the decades of his exile from the human race, he had made love to many mortal women. Usually he had taken their blood and clouded their minds so they wouldn't know.

But not this time. Today he vowed he would take no blood from Emma; he had already taken too much from her.

Her hands drifted upward, pushing up his T-shirt again. He tensed as she stroked his chest, but she made no comment. This time she tugged the shirt up farther, and he yanked it over his head, tossing it onto the floor to join hers.

She smiled at him, continuing to caress his

shoulders, then his chest. "You are so perfect. How can a man be so perfect?" she asked, a note of wonder in her voice. "I want—" The rest of her sentence was lost as he brought his mouth back to hers for a fiery kiss.

When he pulled her closer, they both gave a little cry as the softness of her breasts made contact with the hard planes of his chest. For a long moment, he held her still against him, savoring the warmth of her skin. Then he began to shift her body from side to side, sliding her breasts against his chest.

To his delight, he heard glad little cries tumble from her lips. He felt her knees buckle, but he caught her, supporting her weight.

Her breath came in gasps as he bent her backward, his hands moving to play with her breasts, cup them, shape them to his grasp, tease her nipples to tighter points. The pleasure of touching her that way was almost more than he could stand.

One hand glided to her hips, urging her more firmly against his aching erection, rocking her against him.

Then she was moving on her own, pressing, stroking, frantic for the contact she needed most.

The heat built relentlessly, beyond endurance, and he said her name over and over, telling her how much he wanted her to come undone for him. He felt her melt into a hot, pulsing surge of gratification that brought an incoherent shout to her throat. In the aftermath of her climax, she sagged weakly against him, gasping, her skin slick with perspiration.

He stroked her back, stringing tiny kisses along the side of her face as she dropped her head to his shoulder. When she shivered, he wrapped his arms around her shoulders. His body was rigid, his back still braced against the door.

She raised her face and must have seen the tension burning in his eyes. Slipping her hand between them, she cupped her fingers around his rigid flesh through the shorts they hadn't even removed, stroking his hardness. "I need to feel this inside me."

The breath huffed out of him. He wanted that, too. He wanted everything he could take from her. But he had already taken too much.

"Emma." His mouth came down on hers for a long, greedy kiss. Lifting her into his arms, he carried her to the bed, gently laid her down and swept off her panties. As he gazed down at her, he stripped off his shorts, feeling his erection spring free.

Reaching out, she took him in her hand, stroking her fingers over the hard shaft, drawing a gasp of pleasure from him.

He came down beside her, gathering her close.

Because he wanted this time with her to last as long as he could make it, he started with soft kisses and caresses. Yet very soon, simple kisses and sweet touches weren't enough. One hand left her breasts and slid downward toward the slick heat of her most sensitive flesh. His fingers played over her as they might a fine Stradivarius, wringing exquisite cries of pleasure from her.

Once again, he lifted her higher and higher, until she was writhing and thrusting against his hand.

"Nick...please."

"Oh, yes." He moved over her and plunged into her deeply, his breath coming in gasps as he felt her close tightly around him. Lifting her hips, she surged against him, taking him still deeper.

"Emma!" It seemed he wasn't capable of saying more. Or of pacing himself.

She smoothed her hands over his back, down to his buttocks, pressing him closer. He shifted himself slightly so he could slip a hand between their bellies to stroke her, to stoke her pleasure.

He focused all his concentration on the heat and the friction, on the giving and taking of pleasure. He felt her driving toward completion again—and he felt her take him over the edge.

As she cried out her release, he bent his head, his fangs against the tender flesh of her neck.

Orgasm rocketed through him, but it wasn't

enough. His whole body vibrated with the craving for her blood, and in his mind he could already taste her sweetness. But before his fangs pierced her skin, he forced himself to stop, to remember why he couldn't take her that way. It was too soon. Much too soon.

Calling on every ounce of determination he possessed, he willed his fangs to retract, willed himself to lift his head and take a breath. He felt lost, starving to death in a world where he could never have what he craved.

Her voice brought him back to reality.

"Thank you," she whispered.

He could only nod wordlessly at her astonishing generosity.

As she gazed lovingly up at him, her sky-blue eyes seemed to cloud over. "I thought… Wasn't it good for you, too?"

"It was wonderful," he managed to choke out. "But…?"

He shifted himself off her and gathered her close.

His lips brushed her eyebrows. "But we both need to sleep now."

It was enough that he had satisfied her. Enough that he had climaxed. He told himself that, even though he knew it wasn't true. He was left with an agonizing craving he couldn't allow himself to satisfy.

Another woman would have accepted his re-assurance. Not Emma. "You made that fantastic for me," she murmured. "But something was missing for you."

He couldn't talk about it. Couldn't tell her why his body still throbbed with unfulfilled need.

So he did what he had sworn he wouldn't do. He invaded her mind, soothing her as he helped her slip into sleep.

They were both exhausted. If they slept all day and into the night, that would be good for both of them.

IT HAD INDEED been a good evening thus far, Damien Caldwell thought. Better than he had any right to expect. Nick Vickers had gotten himself shot. Maybe he'd even die from loss of blood. Which would be an excellent resolution to the problem Vickers presented.

To celebrate, Damien sat in his office, contem-plating an extremely pleasurable decision—which one of his women followers to summon to his bed.

He knew their names and faces as well as his own. But he would prolong his own pleasure by making his obsequious male secretary bring him the videotapes, wait for his Master to select the one he desired and then obediently put it into the VCR for the high-definition, wide-screen television set, only to be summarily dismissed before the fun began.

The tapes held Damien's favorite footage from the hidden cameras around the estate. Some of the cameras he used for obvious security purposes. But the ones in the women's dormitories and their bathrooms were strictly for his own private pleasure.

Tonight he had decided to view a tape from the women's shower area. He sat back and watched his male minion find and insert the first tape, bow and wait to be dismissed. "Be gone," Damien instructed the servant brusquely. The man bowed again and scurried out of the room.

Damien smiled as he watched his girls undressing, standing under the shower, bathing their breasts, their buttocks, their intimate places, all the while unsuspecting that he might scrutinize them at will in those most private moments, and from nearly any angle he chose.

It was highly arousing. He watched Kendra Larson get into the shower and raise her arms to shampoo her hair, in the process thrusting her bobbing breasts directly toward the camera.

Then blond, pretty Margaret Birmingham walked into the frame and hurriedly began to take off her nightclothes to get showered and dressed in time for breakfast. She knew he wouldn't abide her being late, and he smiled at this sign of her obedience.

He knew she wasn't trying to be sexy, as she had no idea she was being seen by anyone but the other women moving in and out of the bathroom, but there was an unconscious sensuality about her nonetheless.

He'd had his eye on her for...special purposes for quite a while. He wanted her now, and he thought about summoning her to his bed tonight. She'd come willingly, of course, and she'd serve him in any way he wished. But he knew his own needs. He was too keyed up to settle for mere copulation and a few sips of blood. Whoever came to his bed tonight would die there. And he wanted to keep Margaret around a while longer.

So he enjoyed watching her shower and gave himself over to the pleasure of making his decision.

Whom would he select? And how long would he let her live? Minutes, or hours?

Lately, he'd been killing faster. The craving was getting stronger and stronger. But he dared not let it get out of control. He would put some limits on himself. Or he would have to dredge up a whole new batch of recruits.

EMMA AWOKE feeling groggy. But she knew where she was—in Nicholas Vickers's bed. He had made wonderful love to her. And then... She wasn't sure what had happened after that. She'd felt him climax. Strongly, powerfully. Yet she'd sensed something. Something wrong. She'd been completely, gloriously satisfied. He had seemed restless, unfulfilled. As if he needed something more. But what? Obviously, he wasn't going to tell her.

She sat up cautiously and looked at him. He was sleeping deeply. The covers had slipped down around his waist, and she stared at his chest. This time she didn't make the mistake of touching him. She only leaned over, looking for the indentations in his skin she'd felt after the shoot-out at the crack house in Baltimore. She knew she'd felt something there, and he'd said they were old scars. But as she stared at the broad expanse of his chest, she found nothing out of the ordinary. No scars. No irregularities. Not even a white line. Whatever had been there was gone.

Cautiously, she got out of bed and opened the bathroom door a little wider so that she could see what she was doing. Then she found the Batman T-shirt and panties they'd discarded. After pulling them on, she glanced at Nick again. He hadn't moved, and she suspected he wouldn't wake up unless she touched him again.

Something was out of kilter. Something she needed to figure out, because she knew he wasn't going to explain.

The leather jacket he'd worn to Baltimore was

draped over the back of a chair. She held it up, staring at what certainly looked to be bullet holes in the front *and* back. If they were, he had suffered a couple of through-and-through hits in last night's action. But now he didn't even have a scratch on him.

She noticed a piece of fabric sticking out of the left pocket. She reached in and pulled it out—then stifled a gasp as she held up a sodden black T-shirt. Whatever had spilled onto it was thick, like dried chocolate syrup. But Nick hadn't been in Baltimore to eat an ice-cream sundae.

She set the jacket down and gingerly sniffed the T-shirt. It smelled…coppery, like blood. And it didn't have just a small, damp stain; the shirt was almost completely soaked. The shirt Nick said he hadn't been wearing.

She held it up by the shoulders, and she saw two round holes that let the illumination from the bathroom shine through the fabric.

Her heart pounding, she took a quick glance back at Nick to make sure that he was still sleeping. Then she laid the jacket on the floor and the shirt on top of it. The holes in the two garments lined up perfectly.

Her hand clenched over one leather sleeve. There was no doubt in her mind now. He'd gotten shot at the crack house, all right, and he'd bled profusely. But how…?

She frantically thought back to when she'd found him hiding in the row house cellar. She thought he had been weak. Then...

She struggled to bring the next events into focus, but it was like trying to gather an armful of vapor. All she remembered was finding him and their hiding from the police together. Then they'd come out from the cubbyhole under the cellar stairs, and she'd felt dizzy. She'd had to lean on him as they made their way back to her rental car.

A shiver traveled over her skin. Something had happened in that cellar. Something she didn't understand. Something that terrified her.

But she had to face it.

There were so many things about Nick that she should have thought about more carefully. Little warnings she'd ignored. He'd slept during the day and "worked" all night. Of course, his kind of work *could* dictate such a lifestyle. But no job would explain certain other events.

Such as how he had miraculously, with seemingly supernatural speed and strength, scattered and nearly annihilated the entire gang of would-be arsonists who'd threatened her life and his home. After that, his ministrations had mystifyingly closed her gunshot wound virtually overnight. Then there was tonight, when he had suddenly blocked her exit from his room when she'd thought he was still in his bed.

The word *vampire* hovered in her mind. She tried to force it away, but it kept coming back. And the clincher was what had happened when she'd found him in Baltimore.

She'd gone down there in the first place because she'd thought he was hurt. Then he'd convinced her he was fine. But he'd lied to her about not getting shot. In fact, he'd had bullets go through his chest and out his back. Right in front of her she had the evidence that he had, indeed, bled profusely. Left untended, he surely should have bled to death. But apparently he was now as good as new.

Because?

She shivered, her memory returning. When she'd found him, he'd been weak, hallucinating. From blood loss. But he'd quickly regained his strength, and she'd had no idea how—only that she'd gotten woozy herself and had come out of a "faint" feeling dizzy and weak.

Had he replenished his blood supply from her?

Oh, God. That was why she'd been dizzy. And why he'd insisted on her drinking that potion—*to build up her blood.*

He'd used her for a blood donor, and then… and then his body had healed itself.

A sick feeling rose in her throat.

Nicholas Vickers was a vampire.

And she had made love with him.

She was still closeted in his bedroom with him now.

Her hands squeezed into fists.

Trying to fight down her terror, she dashed toward the door. But before she could leave the room, Nick stirred in the bed.

"Where are you going, Emma?" he asked.

## Chapter Eleven

Emma swallowed hard. If the…the man in the bed figured out she knew his secret, he could probably kill her as easily as he'd squash an ant.

Somehow she managed to speak in an even voice, answering, "I need to use the bathroom."

"Hurry back and keep me warm. There's a good wench."

He was talking like a character from one of his "historical novels" again. Historical novels—hah! Didn't vampires live forever? Weren't they the—she shuddered—"undead"? He'd probably *lived* through those historical eras!

To her vast relief, he made no effort to stop her from leaving the room. Maybe he'd even gone back to sleep, because he couldn't stay awake during the day.

She hurried out of his elegant bedroom suite and into the unfinished part of the basement. Every muscle in her body vibrated with tension as she remembered being trapped like a caged animal on her first trip across that cement floor. No wonder she'd felt as if she were in a house of horrors. She was!

She cringed at that harsh judgment. Yet, it was true, wasn't it?

Had he lied about the alarm system being off? Would he trap her again? No, likely he'd told the truth on that, figuring she might be accustomed to breakfast and lunch and would want something to eat before night fell again and he—it?—arose.

Fighting back tears and sending up a silent prayer, she started across the open space. To her relief, no eerie lights glowed, and no gates crashed down to entrap her.

She didn't want to take the time to go to the bedroom she'd occupied earlier, but she was half-naked, and she didn't want to return to Nick's bedroom. So she dashed up two flights of stairs and pulled on the new slacks she'd purchased.

She had no idea what Nick had done with the gun she'd bought after leaving the Refuge and dropped in his yard. No time to look now. She raced downstairs to the pantry and grabbed one of Nick's.

She was almost ready to leave when she remembered that her car was now in his garage. Which meant that she'd have to go back downstairs.

Teeth clenched, she retraced her steps, expecting that at any moment he might burst out of his bedroom suite and grab her.

But she made it across the basement and then into the garage without incident. She activated the mechanism that opened the door, then gunned her car out into the blessed daylight. The door closed behind her, and she shot down the driveway. She wasn't even sure where she was going. All she could think of was that she'd escaped.

She'd dreamed of Nick Vickers.

She'd felt close to him, even before they met.

Then she met him, trusted him—and made love with him.

She'd been so wrong about Nicholas Vickers. Way, *way* wrong.

But she'd managed to escape him.

So why was she fighting back tears?

She told herself he'd lied to her from the first. He must have. And he'd probably laughed at how easily he'd managed to dupe her into giving him exactly what he wanted from her.

She stopped short, remembering how tenderly he'd cared for her when she was hurt. Dear Lord, he'd healed her after a gunshot wound that could have killed her.

No. She couldn't afford any sentimentality. Vampires probably had mysterious powers to heal humans so they could use them for…for food! She shuddered.

She shuddered harder as another thought hit her. Did vampires also have mysterious powers to draw their prey to them? Is that why she'd felt she *had* to seek out his help to rescue Marg? Had he deliberately sent himself into her dreams, to lure her into coming to him, into trusting him before she'd even met him?

No! It was all too much. And now she was thinking of Nick the way she thought of Damien Caldwell, a weirdo power junkie who used his charisma and strangely compelling powers of persuasion to get people to do his every bidding—and to do so with pleasure.

Oh, God. Strangely compelling powers of persuasion? Was Caldwell a vampire, too?

In the bizarre world she suddenly found herself in, it made perfect sense. They were both vampires.

The two men—monsters?—were, after all, locked in seemingly mortal enmity. Yet with all his own powers, Nick was obviously cautious about going after Caldwell. Did that mean Caldwell had "talents" even Nick didn't possess?

Nick had said Caldwell had had places like the Refuge in the past. Did Caldwell find ways to create his bizarre enclaves so that he would have a constant, ready and willing supply of human blood?

What did Nick do to get blood on a regular basis?

She shook her head violently. She didn't want to know.

But she knew one thing for sure. Caldwell was killing people. Making human sacrifices.

And he had to be stopped. Her thoughts zinged back to Nick. She'd shared his dreams and she'd thought he was the answer to her prayers. What a laugh! She'd always known she was as bad a judge of men as her mother. Either she'd hooked up with a succession of jerks or she'd picked guys who were so bland, they faded into the woodwork.

Well, that certainly wasn't Nick. Not bland at all!

If she hadn't been driving, she would have lowered her head to her hands. As it was, she was forced to keep staring at the taillight of the car ahead of her.

Another man's image leaped into her mind.

Alex Shane.

Alex Shane, the other—the *real*—private detective with an interest in Caldwell's activities. He said he'd been hired to rescue a woman from the Refuge. But would he believe her if she told him Damien Caldwell was a vampire? Or would he cart her off not to Baltimore, but to the loony bin?

Alex would save her. But had she misjudged him, too?

It seemed she'd have to take a chance on that. Because she had just run out of options.

THE PRIVATE LINE on Damien Caldwell's desk rang, and he glanced at the caller ID. It was "Trailblazer," the man he'd had following Nicholas Vickers.

His reports had been useful; the fellow had even called and told him to turn on his TV to catch the breaking news from the Baltimore crack house.

Naturally, Trailblazer was also the one who'd warned the druggies inside that Vickers was sneaking up on them.

Too bad Vickers hadn't died. Apparently he'd managed to recover sufficiently from his injuries to return to his home. Trailblazer had seen him come in just at dawn. Probably with his skin burning.

Snatching up the receiver, Damien said, "Now what? Do you have something more on Vickers?"

"No. But Emma Birmingham just left Vickers's house—on her own."

"Get her. And bring her back here."

HOURS LATER, Nick woke and turned toward Emma. But the bed was empty.

Sitting bolt upright, he fought off a surge of panic. She was probably upstairs, getting something to eat. His gaze went to the clock on the wall. It was only a little after nine, early in the evening.

He jumped out of bed and pulled on his jeans. As he did, he saw the jacket he'd left on the chair. The bloody shirt was sticking halfway out of the pocket.

Staring at it, he went cold all over. Had Emma seen it? If she had, she'd have known instantly that he'd been lying to her. And she was smart enough to put two and two together and figure out he'd been lying to her all along, about a lot of things.

Hoping he was wrong, afraid that he wasn't, he searched his private quarters, then dashed up the stairs. She wasn't in the kitchen, the living room or any other room.

She was gone. She'd run away from him—because she'd figured out the deep dark secret he'd been hiding.

And he knew where she was going. He'd come to understand her well enough to be certain she wouldn't abandon her sister to Damien Caldwell.

So she was running from one vampire into the arms of another. He wondered if she knew it. Could she have figured out that Caldwell, too, was a blood drinker?

It didn't matter. The only thing that concerned him was how much of a head start she had—and how much chance he had of stopping her before she put her life in jeopardy.

Quickly, he finished dressing, then checked the contents of a knapsack that he kept packed for emergencies. It had sunscreen, protective clothing, binoculars and a few other useful items. From a locked drawer in his office, he got one more thing, something he'd been planning to take with him to the Refuge, even before Emma Birmingham had come asking for his help.

The idea of driving into Caldwell's lair made his blood run cold. Long ago, when he'd gone up against the monster, he'd barely escaped with his life. Then he had been fighting to avenge Jeanette's death. Over the years, though, his motivation for destroying Caldwell had changed. He was determined to stop the demon's killing spree.

He'd known a direct assault on his archenemy would only get him killed. In the past hundred and fifty years, he'd tried five stealth attacks. All had failed because Caldwell had made himself almost invincible.

So Nick had gone back to the drawing board, using the considerable skill he'd developed as an engineer. Finally, he had invented a weapon he believed would eliminate the Master—*believed* being the operative word. There was no way to test the weapon. He had to get it right the first time or die trying.

He glanced at the clock again. Most likely, Emma had left when she'd said she was going to use the bathroom and he'd fallen back asleep. She was hours ahead of him. Yet he had to assume she wasn't reckless enough to try to sneak into Caldwell's compound in broad daylight. Which gave him a chance to find her before she tried to go in on her own.

If she did, she'd surely get caught, and it made him sick with fear to think that the silly chit might just be foolish—and desperate—enough to try it.

Cursing the woman who had fled his protection, he stepped into his garage and threw his knapsack into the backseat of his Acura. It was a fast car, with an engine he'd had supercharged for emergencies. Usually he didn't chance speeding. Tonight was the exception. His lips set in a grim line, he turned on the radar detector—another modern convenience that he greatly appreciated—and roared out of the garage.

IT WAS AFTER MIDNIGHT, and only a few lights shone in the windows of St. Stephens when Emma drove into town. The highway turned into Main Street, which was lined on both sides with real estate offices, art and craft galleries, clothing boutiques and restaurants.

She'd come here because she had nowhere else to go. She couldn't simply run home with her tail between her legs and leave Margaret to die. Yet now that she was within striking distance of the Refuge, she was filled with uncertainty.

When she'd left Nick's house, she'd told herself she could ask Alex Shane for help. As her fingers closed around his business card, she felt a pang of guilt. It was bad enough asking him to go to the Refuge when she thought Damien Caldwell was a man. Now that she was convinced he was a vampire, she simply couldn't do it. Shane had told her about his wife and kids and how he wasn't free to take the same kind of risks that he'd taken when he was a bachelor. No, in good conscience, she couldn't ask him to go with her to the Refuge.

But he'd said he worked for the Light Street Detective Agency. Maybe they could put together a larger force, enough people who knew how to handle themselves, so that they'd stand a chance against Caldwell and his guards.

She argued back and forth with herself for several minutes, then headed for the dock in the center of town, where people congregated and she wouldn't be alone. Pulling up beside the public phone that sat outside the dockside restaurant, she looked around. Another car had stopped nearby, and she saw a man watching her.

Did he know who she was? Maybe he simply wanted to use the same phone.

He looked away, but he'd given her a bad feeling that made her reluctant to climb out of her car. While she debated what to do, two couples walked out of the restaurant together. Rolling down her window, she called to them.

"Pardon me. I need some help." When the couples stopped, she gave what she hoped was an embarrassed sort of smile. "The truth is, I'm having a fight with my boyfriend, and I need to make sure he's not going to leap out of the bushes when I get home—or leap out of the bushes here, for that matter. I wondered if you'd watch my car for just a minute, while I make a phone call?"

"Sure thing," one of the men said.

"Thanks a million." Emma climbed out of the car, strode to the phone and dialed Alex Shane's number.

To her relief, he answered on the second ring.

"Shane here."

Though his voice sounded crisp, she suspected that she'd awakened him.

"This is Emma Birmingham. I'm sorry to call so late."

"No problem. What's up?"

"I…" She looked back at the couple who'd agreed to watch her car. "I can't talk long, but I need to see you. Can you meet me at the place where you...ran into me the other night?"

"Where are you now?"

"I'd rather not say."

"Okay. Give me a minute." He was silent for several seconds, then said, "I'll meet you a hundred yards from where we met the first time. A hundred yards closer to town. You know where I mean?"

"Yes. Thanks."

"I'll be there in fifteen minutes."

She exited the phone booth and thanked the couple for watching her car. Then she drove away.

Instead of making right for the spot where Alex was going to meet her, she circled around town, watching her rearview as she drove. It didn't look like anyone was behind her, but she spent several more minutes making unnecessary turns, traveling sidestreets and alleyways through St. Stephens, before heading toward the road along the river.

WHEN THE PHONE rang again, Damien snatched it up even quicker than before. "You have her."

Trailblazer hesitated.

"Spit it out."

"She gave me the slip."

"You moron."

"Do you have any men on this side of the river?"

"Of course."

"Well, tell them to be on the lookout for her."

"I will," he growled, thinking about how he was going to punish his operative for screwing this up—if the man was stupid enough to return.

EMMA LOOKED FOR a place to park. She could have pulled onto the shoulder, but leaving the car in the open didn't seem like a great idea. So she drove slowly down the two-lane highway until she found an old side road where she could pull off into the woods. It wasn't perfect, but it was the best she could do.

Once she'd gotten out, she looked around. It was pitch-dark, not a streetlight in sight, isolated, scary. To add to the eerie atmosphere, a low-lying mist was drifting up from the river to cover the road. It was the perfect spot for an ambush—if anyone had spotted her in town and followed her.

With a shiver, she reached into her purse and retrieved the gun she'd taken from Nick's pantry. The cold metal felt reassuring in her hand. She'd never shot at a living creature, but she was an excellent shot on the practice range. She knew how to handle the weapon, and she kept it down by her right leg, with her arm straight, as she started up the road toward the spot that Alex had indicated.

Her footsteps rang hollowly on the blacktop.

Then she thought she heard a crunching sound behind her. Whirling, she raised the gun, but she saw no one.

"Get a grip," she muttered as she started up the road again. But now she felt the hairs prickling at the back of her neck. With the gun clutched in her hand, she picked up her pace, then darted into the woods. It was dark under the trees, and something clawed at the legs of her slacks. Brambles, she told herself. Only brambles.

She yanked her leg away and kept going. Straining her ears, she heard it again—the sound of someone or something behind her.

Praying that Alex would come along soon, she quickened her steps. But she'd gotten only another few feet when a pair of arms grabbed her around the neck and waist, cutting off her air and clamping her gun hand to her thigh.

"Scream and you'll be sorry," a man's voice said as he brought her left arm up at an angle that sent pain shooting through her shoulder.

She went very still.

"That's right. Come along nice and easy."

She recognized the voice. It was a guy named Gordo, one of the men who worked for Caldwell. Silently, she cursed herself for coming back to the river road. It looked like Caldwell had men patrolling the area. Maybe even looking specifically for her.

He held her fast, twisting her left arm behind her back. He hadn't yet realized, though, that she had a gun in her right hand. Unfortunately, she couldn't get off a shot at anything but the ground.

"Please, you're hurting me," she moaned, still playing for time.

"Shut up!"

When he jerked on her arm, she fought not to scream in pain.

Despite his superior size and strength, she vowed she wasn't going to go down without a fight. Because there was nothing else she could do, she went limp. Gordo lost his footing on the slick road, which gave her the chance to duck down and raise the gun. But he was back on her before she could catch her breath, cursing as he lashed out an arm and smacked her across the face.

She gasped from the pain as her teeth cut the inside of her lip.

He grabbed her gun hand, keeping the gun barrel pointed toward the ground. "Drop it, before I break your arm."

She wasn't about to follow orders. If she could just get the gun up into firing position, she still had a chance....

A chance she never got.

Out of the night, a whirlwind materialized, shooting past and knocking both her and Gordo to the ground. He screamed in terror, and so did she as a force she couldn't see lifted Gordo into the air and tossed him into the woods like a sack of garbage. Then a blur took off after him, something moving so fast that she still wasn't sure what was happening.

Gordo screamed again, then the night fell silent. As she watched in fascination, a figure emerged from the woods and started toward her.

She stared in disbelief. "Nick, is that you?"

"You're bloody right it's me. Did you think I'd let you face Caldwell by yourself?" Before she could answer, he plowed on. "And you're damned lucky I found you. What the bloody hell do you think you're doing?"

As he stalked toward her, she raised her chin—and the gun.

NICK TOOK note of the gun in Emma's hand and kept walking.

"I see you're not afraid of getting shot," she said sarcastically. "But then, why should you be? You got shot in Baltimore. You should be dead. And don't hand me that crap about the bullets missing you. I saw the shirt."

When he was within five feet of her, she took a few backward steps. "Get away from me, you…vampire!"

Nick halted. The word hung in the air between them for a long moment.

"Emma," he said quietly, "did I ever hurt you?"

"You took blood from me!" she cried.

He winced, feeling her anger and sense of betrayal. "If I hadn't, I'd have died." He thought it best not to mention the other times he'd sampled the nectar that ran in her veins.

"I *trusted* you."

"Keep trusting me," he said, hearing the gritty sound of his own voice.

"How can I?"

"Because I'd die myself before I'd let anyone hurt you. And if you need a more concrete reason, because I just saved you from one of Caldwell's thugs. And because I have a plan to save your sister."

She eyed him suspiciously. "Why should I believe you?"

"Why shouldn't you? Why would I be here at all if I weren't sincere? Why would I have bothered to follow you?"

"Every time I asked you to help me, you said you'd think about it," she accused.

"I've tried five times to attack Caldwell. He's fought me off every time."

She winced.

"I have a new plan."

"What?"

"I'd rather not talk about it here."

With a sigh, she lowered the gun, but when he

took a step toward her, she backed away. "Don't come near me. Please."

"Okay," he agreed, though he longed to fold her into his arms and hold her tight. "Are you all right?"

"I think so."

Before she could say more, headlights blinked on behind her. Nick threw up his arm to protect his eyes from the sudden painful glare.

Damn! While they'd been standing here arguing, Caldwell had sent reinforcements.

## Chapter Twelve

Whirling toward the headlights, Emma raised her gun straight at them.

"Don't shoot," said a steel-edged voice from the car belonging to the lights.

Relief came like a stiff breeze blowing off the water.

"Alex," she said.

"Yeah. Were you planning to lure me here and drill me?"

"Oh Lord, I'm so sorry."

"I'm kidding. I hope." He got out of the car and stepped around where she could see him in the twin beams. He was also armed, and his gaze was fixed on Nick as he asked, "Is this guy giving you any trouble?"

"No, he…" She shot Nick a quick glance. "He knocked out one of Caldwell's men."

Nick stepped forward. "And you are…?"

"Alex Shane."

"A private detective who's worked on the Eastern Shore for the past three years," Nick supplied.

"And I assume you're Nicholas Vickers, a P.I. who works in the Baltimore-Howard County area."

"Correct."

Emma watched the two men sizing each other up.

"You're a little far from home," Alex said.

"I followed Emma down here," Nick replied. "How did you end up on this stretch of road in the middle of the night?"

"Emma called me."

"I see." Nick fixed his gaze on her. "And what were you planning to tell him?"

She licked suddenly dry lips. She'd intended to tell Alex Shane that Caldwell was a vampire. Suddenly that didn't seem like such a smart idea. The explanation had been so vivid in her mind. Now it just sounded delusional.

"I was hoping he could help me figure out a way to get Margaret out of there," she said in a small voice.

Nick held her gaze a moment longer, then turned his attention to Alex. With a nod toward the vehicle in the middle of the road, he said, "You'd better pull onto the shoulder and shut off those headlights, before someone wonders what's going on."

"What about Caldwell's man?" Alex asked. "Is he in any shape to come after us?"

"Not unless he's Houdini. I tied him up pretty tightly."

Alex returned to his car and climbed inside. As soon as he started down the road, Nick turned back to her.

"Were you planning to tell him about me?"

"No!" Emma exclaimed.

He was silent for a moment, his expression unreadable in the darkness. "I'd like to talk you out of going in there tonight," he said finally. "But if Caldwell knows you're in the area, he may go after your sister in retaliation."

Before she could answer, Alex came walking back toward them, looking uncertain.

"Is rushing over there tonight the best plan?" he asked. "Why don't we wait until tomorrow, until we can collect some reinforcements."

Nick shook his head. "We were just talking about that. Given that his guard was waiting for her, we have to assume Caldwell knows Emma is here and that she was planning to try to rescue her sister. We also have to assume he'll soon know his goon failed to snatch her. Which means Margaret is at risk—tonight."

"Yeah," Alex conceded. "But I don't like letting you go over there alone."

Emma jumped in. "You can't come with us, not

after what you told me about your wife not wanting you to take risks. I'd never forgive myself if you got into trouble on my account."

Alex gave her a considering look. "What about if *you* get into trouble?"

"If you don't hear from us in three hours, call the cops," Nick answered.

Alex sighed heavily. "Okay. I guess that's the best we can do."

As the two men exchanged looks, she wondered if either one of them believed that a rescue operation could work. Before Alex could make any objections, she said, "We should go. Do you have a boat?"

"Yeah, I do."

He led them down the road several hundred feet, where an aluminum rowboat was hidden in a clump of marsh grass and cattails.

"I've used it to row over a couple of times," Alex said.

"What if you don't get it back?" Nick asked.

Alex shrugged. "The Light Street Detective Agency can take it as an insurance loss."

Emma worked her way through the exchange. If they didn't return the boat it would be because they were dead.

Alex pulled the rowboat out of its camouflage, then held the rope while Nick helped her in. She settled in the bow, and Nick climbed in after her, taking the middle seat.

As he reached for the oars, she felt a shiver go through her. Until this moment, she hadn't thought about the implications of being alone with him again.

With a quiet "Good luck," Alex gave them a hefty shove away from shore.

Nick began rowing. She watched him, silence stretching between them. Then, about fifty yards from shore, he stopped rowing. The boat glided a few feet, then was caught by the current and began to drift.

"What are you doing?" she asked. "Double-crossing me?"

NICK SIGHED as he watched the nervous tension gather in Emma's face. "No double cross," he said. "We have to talk before we do this."

"About what?" she challenged.

He rested his arms on the oars, keeping his gaze steady on her. "Can I assume you've deduced that Caldwell is a vampire?"

"Yes."

"Well, then, perhaps you also understand why I wasn't eager to dash to your sister's rescue. I'm a realist, Emma. Caldwell is many centuries older than I am, and a lot stronger. He's also devious in a way that I am not, regardless of what you might believe."

She gave a small, one-shouldered shrug and an even smaller nod.

Well, he thought, that was something.

He continued. "Caldwell uses his personal magnetism—and I'll grant that he does have that—as well as his vampiric powers to gather people to him. As I'm sure you must realize, those people are nothing more than food to him."

Her hands were clamped over the gunwales, as though to steady herself. And her upset could only get worse. The truth was brutal, but she needed to know it. All of it.

"I told you that I was one of the Master's trusted inner circle." Nick paused, then added, "That was in 1852."

He heard her suck in a breath.

Resolutely, he continued. "I thought he was a great leader. I helped defend his castle against a horde of villagers who were desperate to kill the vampire lording it over their land. I was mortally wounded in the attack. He told me that he could save me, but that it would mean becoming like him. I didn't understand what that meant at first. But I learned. And for a while it was true—I was exactly like him. I fed on humans, as he did, and it didn't occur to me to do otherwise."

Unable to bear the revulsion on Emma's face,

Nick shifted his gaze to the moonlit surface of the river. Forcing himself to keep going, he said, "When Jeanette joined the enclave, everything changed. She was good and innocent, and loving her reminded me of my humanity, which made me see what a monster Damien Caldwell was— and what a monster I myself had become."

Shooting Emma a quick glance, he muttered, "I'm no paragon, but I've tried to use my life—my knowledge and skills, including my enhanced abilities—if not for good, at least in a way that does no harm. I stopped draining the blood from mortals before Caldwell killed Jeanette. These days, I feed on the deer that live in the woods around my house."

He gave a harsh laugh. "I'd go into a full recitation of my good works, but we'd better get back to Caldwell."

Returning his gaze to Emma, hoping it wasn't merely wishful thinking that she looked slightly less revolted, he said, "Unfortunately, there's no way we can simply march into the Refuge and get to your sister. Caldwell has too many loyal followers and, as you know, plenty of guards."

"Then…" She looked toward the far shore, then back at him. "What are we going to do?"

"Kill Caldwell."

She looked thunderstruck. "You mean drive an oak stake through his heart?"

"That's the traditional method, although any

sort of stake will do, as long as it causes all the blood to drain from the body. But Caldwell is hardly going to stand still for it."

"So…"

"I've been developing a weapon that I think will kill him." He reached into his knapsack and took out the small object he'd brought along.

Emma looked at the black tube, which had a glass-covered light at one end. "You're going to kill him with a flashlight?"

Nick suppressed a smile. "It's a laser gun."

"Like in *Star Trek?*"

At that, he couldn't help but chuckle. "Right, and I'm James T. Kirk, so of course, Caldwell doesn't stand a chance against me. A million to one odds are nothing to me."

"That much, I believe," she whispered.

Nick sobered. "Emma, I can only try to—"

"You do have a better chance against him than anybody else," she said, "because no one could possibly understand him better than you do."

They stared at each other for a long moment, and he knew quite well what she'd left unsaid: She realized why he was the best one, maybe the only one, who could destroy the Master. But that didn't mean she trusted him or wanted to be near him. On a personal level, the jury was still out— and it didn't look to him as if the verdict was going to be in his favor.

Nick got on with the business at hand. "I told you I designed video games. But this laser isn't a toy." He pointed the business end at the water and pressed the button on the side. A beam of red light shot out of the front, and where it hit the river, the water sizzled and boiled. After several seconds, he switched it off.

Emma looked from the water to the weapon, then to him. "That's amazing."

He hefted the tool in his hand. "It's also dangerous. The beam will cut through flesh and bone."

Her eyes widened. "Have you tested it?"

"On roadkill."

As he watched her try to wipe that image from her mind, he hurried on. "I was in the process of designing a safety catch, but you arrived on my doorstep and, since then, there hasn't been time to work on it. Just don't press the button accidentally. Here—" Holding the weapon so that it pointed at the water, he leaned forward to hand it to her.

She drew back. "You want *me* to use it?"

"It makes sense. No, wait—listen to me. Caldwell will be *expecting* an attack from me, which means I can distract him. And while he's focused on me, with some luck, you'll be in a position to use the laser. Just make sure you aim for the heart."

She was silent a moment, chewing on her full bottom lip. "What if he doesn't come after you?"

Nick snorted. "Believe me, he will. Our mutual hatred is long-standing and very personal. He'll go after me. And you'll go after him. And when he's out of the way, you'll get Margaret out of there, then call the police."

"But they'll arrest me for killing him."

Nick shook his head. "There won't be any evidence. If Caldwell is left in direct sunlight, his body will incinerate."

"I thought he could tolerate sunlight," Emma said, frowning.

"He can, because he uses a kind of mind control over the cells of his body. But once he's dead, his power will cease to exist."

Still suspicious, she asked, "How do you know?"

He shrugged. "I read about it."

"But isn't the stuff written about vampires a bunch of myths?"

"Most of it, yes. But there are some authoritative texts. In limited editions, of course. They're written by vampires."

"Why would they write about themselves?"

He shrugged. "Lots of reasons, I suppose. The need to communicate, to tell their stories, to help other vampires…just to brag?" He shrugged again. "Why does anyone write a book?"

She was playing with the string tie of her loosefitting slacks, her gaze directed at her lap. "You've met them? These other vampires?"

He hesitated, then nodded. How odd it felt to admit these things, to talk freely about what he was. He had never told anyone, not a single soul, and frankly, doing so terrified him. He was handing Emma the power to destroy his life—perhaps to destroy him. But he wanted her to know the truth because...

Because he loved her. He loved her as he had never loved any other woman.

She had fled from him, frightened by half truths and myths, hurt and justifiably angry that he'd lied to her. He didn't doubt for an instant that she would run away again. But at least she would know the truth. He hoped she might someday come to understand him and his life and why he had lied in an effort to protect her—and himself. He had to admit that part.

But she didn't know how much he ached to have everything be different. He had pictured the two of them living a normal life. Husband and wife. Making love at night. Getting up in the morning together. Raising children together. When he thought about everything that he could never have with her, he felt a giant hole open up in his heart.

But he kept that secret sorrow locked away.

He couldn't burden her with any of his own terrible longings.

And he was certain she already understood that he could never be the lover, the mate, she needed and deserved to have.

Careful to keep his inner turmoil out of his voice, he answered her question. "The only other vampire I've known well is Caldwell. But I've met some who've formed covens. Most, like me, seem to prefer living alone."

She shot him a glance from under lowered lashes. "Where are these books you've read?"

"In my library."

"I didn't see them."

He gave a small, crooked smile. "I keep the good stuff locked up in the cabinet behind the globe." His hands tightened on the oars again. "We can talk more about this later, if you're interested. And if we get out of the Refuge in one piece."

Her head snapped up, all the courage and determination he so admired in her coming to the fore. "We will," she insisted.

"I hope so." He didn't dare hope, however, that she'd ever again give him the chance to be with her.

He resumed rowing. "So we're agreed on our strategy?"

"Do I have a choice?"

"Not unless you've got a better plan."

She sighed, then shook her head.

"All right, then."

EMMA WATCHED Nick row, his steady strokes taking them toward the edge of the estate, inside the razorwire–topped electric fence but not close enough to it to set off the alarms. She couldn't deny that seeing his well-muscled shoulders and arms work the oars caused a fluttering warmth in her belly. It would have been a pleasure simply to watch his athletic performance if the circumstances hadn't been so dire.

And if she weren't so numb with shock from the things he'd told her. She had to keep reminding herself that he was here to help her, that he had no reason at all to hurt her, that if he'd wanted to hurt her, *seriously* hurt her, he could have done so long before now. And yet…he was a vampire.

A *vampire!*

Could she *ever* trust him, truly and completely? Suppose she put aside the lies he'd told her to protect his identity, which she might—might!— forgive. Could she be certain he wouldn't lie about other, far more important things? Things like whether or not he would ever give in to the temptation to drink her blood?

Things like whether or not he'd ever join forces again with Damien Caldwell?

The two hated each other *now*. But by his own admission, Nick had once been in the Master's thrall. She had seen firsthand what Caldwell could do to a person's mind. Could Nick truly promise that he'd never again succumb to his former Master's power?

She had no idea, none at all. And here she was, trapped in a boat with him, heading straight for Caldwell's lair.

Looking up, she caught him staring at her.

"Are you all right?" he asked, his tone concerned, as if he truly cared about her.

"Yes," she replied, even though she felt as if she were in the midst of the worst possible nightmare.

About fifteen feet from the shore, Nick hopped over the side into the knee-deep water, took hold of the bowline and hauled the rowboat onto the beach. The hull scraping against the sand was the only sound in the still, dark night.

After grabbing his knapsack, he helped her out. She waited on the narrow strip of sand as he pushed the rowboat back into the water and guided it a few yards away into a clump of tall grass. When he returned to her, he handed her the laser gun again.

This time, she took it.

"Stuff it into your waistband," he said, "until you need it."

She did as he asked, but she also pulled out the handgun she'd taken from his pantry. It might take a laser to kill Caldwell, but his guards weren't immune to bullets.

"Ready?" he whispered.

She nodded. "Let's go."

ALEX SHANE sat in his home office in the dark. When the door behind him opened, he saw Sara slip into the room.

"You should be sleeping," he murmured.

"I heard you come in. When you didn't come up to bed, I knew there must be something on your mind."

"Yeah."

"What happened with that woman who called?"

"I let her go off to the Refuge."

She gave him a startled look. "Alone?"

"No. With Nicholas Vickers."

"And you think they're going to get into trouble?" When he didn't answer, she added, "Maybe you'd better call in the troops."

"If I do, our people could get hurt."

"And if you don't, other people could get killed."

"Yeah."

EMMA CLIMBED the short bank from the beach and started to follow Nick across the lawn, toward the mansion. They hadn't gone more than five yards when a sharp command stopped them.

"Drop your weapons. Put your hands in the air and turn around slowly."

With her heart pounding in her throat, Emma dropped the handgun immediately, but before she raised her arms, she managed to shove the laser down inside the front of her pants. Then, hands in the air, she started to turn.

She didn't even see Nick fly past her. One instant he was in front of her, and the next instant, he was behind the guard, the side of his hand chopping down hard on the goon's neck.

The man went down, sprawled on the crabgrass.

"The safest thing would be to drown this guy," Nick muttered. "But once Caldwell is dead, the cretin may revert to a reasonable human being, depending on what he was like before the Master took over his mind." As he spoke, he got more cord from his knapsack and a gag. In a couple of minutes, their captive was stowed beside the rowboat, hidden by the tall grass.

"We'll circle around and approach the house from the side," Nick whispered. Then, suddenly, he stopped and pressed his hand to his forehead.

"What?" she asked.

"I…" He never finished the sentence.

Emma watched in horror as he sank to his knees. "Nick!"

She dropped down beside him as he doubled over, then fell to his side, still holding his head, gasping in pain.

"Nick! What is it? Tell me how to help you!"

"That's quite beyond your powers," a deep voice said from out of the darkness.

She recognized that voice. It was Damien Caldwell.

He continued in a conversational tone. "I'm afraid he's suffering from a touch of mind control. He's been practicing techniques to repel me, but they'll do him no good." Caldwell shook his head. "No good at all."

## Chapter Thirteen

Nick couldn't move. He lay on his side, horrible images flashing through his mind. His worst nightmares. Caldwell dragging Jeanette off to her death. Emma lying pale and lifeless on the beach.

He gasped and tried to reach toward her. But his muscles wouldn't work.

Deep in his brain, he knew what was happening to him, but he simply couldn't block the Master's far more powerful thoughts from taking control of him. The endless years of practice had been wasted. He'd been a fool to think he'd ever be able to beat Caldwell at his own game.

Six guards came out of the woods, and it filled him with despair and rage when two of them rolled Emma over and cuffed her hands behind her back. The sight of her lying helpless at Caldwell's feet made his stomach roil. The only consolation was that he knew she wasn't dead.

Growling, he tried to push himself up, but Caldwell kicked him back to the ground.

Powerless to prevent it, he lay on the sand as a guard cuffed him. The bond shouldn't have held him for two seconds, but with Caldwell neutralizing his vampiric powers, he couldn't summon the strength to get free.

The guards hauled him to his feet.

"Take the man to my office and the woman to a holding cell," Caldwell ordered.

"No!" Shouting that one word took every ounce of effort Nick could summon. His knees buckled, and he would have fallen to the ground again if the two guards hadn't been holding him.

"Bind the man to the metal chair in my office," Caldwell directed. "Use the heaviest restraints. I'll take care of him later."

"Yes, sir."

The two guards hustled him off. The last sight he had of Emma was Caldwell leaning over her, grinning.

He felt sick and weak as the guards dragged him to the Master's office, then used massive iron shackles around his ankles and a chain running between them, which they ran through the legs of the chair. Once his legs were secure, they replaced the handcuffs with wrist manacles, which they chained to steel bolts built into the chair arms. Then they searched him and found nothing, because Emma had the laser gun. Not for long, though; they were bound to search her, too.

The guards left him, and he sat manacled to the chair, cursing his stupidity. He should have known his efforts to improve his mental defenses would be worthless without an enemy against whom he could practice. Still, it had shocked him how easily Caldwell had disarmed him and scrambled his thoughts. When Emma had come to him, pleading for help, he'd been worried that he wasn't entirely ready—but not so worried that he hadn't let her persuade him to bring her here. His naiveté—no, his arrogance—had sealed her fate, as well as his own.

He listened for footsteps outside the door, but he was utterly alone for a long time, thinking about what Caldwell was doing, trying futilely to block the images from his mind.

At least he didn't feel quite so ill. As he felt his strength slowly returning, he tested his recovery by pulling against his chains. They were strong, too strong for him in his current state. Caldwell had cut him off at the knees, and he didn't think he stood a chance of summoning the necessary mental energy to change the molecules of the metal in time to do any good.

Finally, after what felt like centuries, the

Master stepped into the room. He stood for a long moment, staring at his prisoner, a small satisfied smile flickering around his lips.

"At last, we meet again," he said.

Nick didn't bother to return the greeting.

"Clever little Emma Birmingham brought you to me."

He pressed his lips together, unwilling to dignify the boast with a reply. "You think I meant that I used the sister as bait to draw her—and you—to me, don't you? Well, you're wrong. Emma has been working for me."

Nick's gaze snapped upward, focusing on Caldwell's face.

"She's a good actress, don't you think? All sweet and innocent like your precious Jeanette. I imagine she convinced you that she cared about your worthless hide."

Nick spoke through gritted teeth. "Is there a point to your lies?"

The Master chuckled. "It was all a carefully orchestrated plan, starting with that gang of repellent bikers and ending with the little drama at the crack house."

Nick snorted, unwilling to let Caldwell know that he was the least disconcerted by the extent of the Master's information about him.

"My man arranged for Miss Birmingham to arrive at your quaint home at just the right time."

"In time to get shot. Oh, certainly. She'd have agreed to that."

Caldwell grinned nastily. "I didn't say that she knew she would be shot or that she had *agreed* to anything. Not in the conscious sense, at any rate."

Walking to a large cabinet on the wall opposite Nick's chair, Caldwell opened the doors to reveal a television screen and a combo DVD/VCR player. Slotting a tape into the machine, he turned, giving Nick another nasty grin.

"I apologize for the poor tape quality," he said. "It was made by a surveillance camera. But, well, I believe you'll get the picture." Then he punched the Play button.

The TV screen came to life. The setting, Nick observed, was this room—Caldwell's office. A man and a woman were standing by the window, talking. The man was Caldwell, and the woman was…Emma.

Caldwell spoke first. "You're going to help me trap Nicholas Vickers."

She wrung her hands together nervously. "But, Master, I don't want to leave the Refuge. I don't want to leave you."

It was Emma's voice. Nick had heard that voice too often not to recognize it. Nor could he have failed to recognize the silky blond hair and nicely rounded figure, clothed in linen slacks and a soft pink blouse.

But then…maybe it *wasn't* Emma. She and her sister were twins. She'd never said they were identical twins, but they could be—and even if they weren't, they could look very much alike.

"Don't worry, my dear," Caldwell said to her in his most charming tone. "You won't be gone for long. Like others I send out to work for our greater cause, you, too, will serve and be rewarded."

"I understand, Master."

His insides in turmoil, Nick told himself, *It's Margaret, not Emma. It can't be Emma….*

But then Caldwell turned the woman toward him, raising her face to his with a finger under her chin. "Now look at me and listen carefully," he ordered. And Nick's heart sank like a stone.

"You want to rescue your sister Margaret," the Master told his servant. "And you need Nicholas Vickers's help. You searched my office and found a file all about Vickers, and the papers in the file make it clear that he's my enemy."

He was planting the message in her mind. The spoken words were merely for show. Nick had seen the Master in action too often—had been his victim too often—not to know that as he spoke, Caldwell was programming Emma's mind to do his bidding.

And, yes, it must be Emma. Exactly as he had feared when she arrived on his doorstep, she had been acting on Caldwell's orders. Everything she'd said and done, everything that had passed between them had been a sham.

"You tried to get Margaret to leave with you," Caldwell continued. "But she refused to go. You desperately need Nicholas Vickers to help you rescue your poor deluded sister."

"Yes, Master. I need his help."

"Yes, and you will do whatever is necessary to secure it. You will charm him, as I know you can. You will make love with him, if it serves the cause. You will do anything—anything at all—to persuade him to come with you to the Refuge. Do you understand?"

"Yes, Master."

"Good."

If he had been human, Nick thought he might have thrown up; he felt that sick. Then Caldwell drew Emma into his arms and made everything much, much worse.

He bent to kiss her slender neck, his hand lifting to stroke her breast. She arched into the caress, moaning in a way that said she welcomed her Master's touch.

"Do you want to make love with me again?" he asked.

"Oh, yes. The last time was so wonderful."

When Caldwell began unbuttoning her blouse, Nick knew he'd have to close his eyes. He couldn't continue to sit here, stony-faced, pretending indifference, when every cell in his body was howling in pain and fury.

Then the screen turned to fuzz, the scene over. But any relief he might have felt was blotted out by the look of triumph on Caldwell's face. The bastard knew he had hated every torturing second of the tape.

He turned his head away, thinking it was too much to hope that Caldwell might leave him alone now.

He was right not to hope. The Master wasn't finished with him.

"Sit here and contemplate that for a while. I'm going to get Emma ready. She thinks she's going to be rewarded for having fulfilled my wishes. She doesn't know that her reward will be to star in one of my ceremonies."

Nick's head jerked up, his gaze fastening on Caldwell's.

"And you, Nicholas, will have a front-row seat, just as in the good old days. So, you see, you'll get your revenge. You'll watch Emma die. After that I'll tie you to a table and let the sun burn you to cinders. Then, at last, I'll be rid of you."

"Did you send me the dreams, too?" Nick asked.

"The dreams." Caldwell looked momentarily

startled. "Yes," he answered. Then, with a final smirk, he left, closing the door solidly behind him.

IN HER CELL, Emma remained silent, cringing inwardly, as a guard performed a rough body search on her. But when he started to investigate the front of her slacks, she figured she had nothing to lose by asserting her feminine modesty.

Pushing his hand away, she whispered, "Please, not there. Besides," she added, thinking a little reminder of his position wouldn't hurt, "you know the Master doesn't like another man touching what he considers his."

To her amazement, it worked. The guard hesitated, then apparently decided she was right and respected her privacy. So the laser gun stayed where she had concealed it, shoved into her underpants, beneath the loose-fitting slacks.

The guard then threw her onto a bench and chained her hands, still cuffed behind her back, to a ring in the wall beside her. With a satisfied grunt, he left her.

She huddled on the bench, her gaze taking in her very limited surroundings. The cell was in a cinder block building away from the main house. The one small window in the outer wall was secured by bars. So was the small window in the door. She could feel the laser gun pressing against her abdomen, but she couldn't get to it.

Overwhelmed by despair and fear, she tried to ease the pain in her arms by bending her elbows and leaning against the wall. Nick had warned her not to return. She hadn't listened. And here she was, chained and helpless. Plus, in her ill-planned rush to get Margaret out of Caldwell's clutches, she'd delivered Nick to him on the proverbial silver platter. Taken by surprise, Nick hadn't even had a chance to fight back before Caldwell had laid him out like a beached fish.

So now they would all die—she and Nick and, eventually, Margaret, whenever Caldwell decided he wanted her blood more than he wanted her accounting skills.

"Great going, Em," she muttered. "Really great."

When she heard the footsteps of a large man outside, she tensed. A key rattled in the lock, and Caldwell stepped into the room and closed the door behind him.

As always, his sheer size was intimidating. He was at least six-four or -five, with a powerful chest and massive arms and legs. Her gaze flicked to his mouth, then away, but she couldn't stop the pictures playing in her mind—pictures of scenes from vampire movies—with Caldwell standing in for the villain.

For a long moment, he simply stared at her.

Then he took a few strolling steps toward her. "So, did Mr. Vickers tell you what I am?" he asked.

"Wh-what do you mean?" she countered, unable to keep her voice steady.

"Ah, Miss Birmingham, don't insult my intelligence, and I won't insult yours. You know what I mean. And I believe you know that I'm a vampire." Closing the short distance between them in two quick strides, he grabbed her chin and tipped her face toward his. "A real vampire. Not one of those role players who hang out in Goth clubs."

He opened his mouth in a parody of a grin, and as she watched in sickened fascination, his teeth changed. Behind the canine teeth, two long white points emerged. He bent toward her, and she tried to wrench away. He easily held her fast, but he only pressed the sharp teeth to her neck before he straightened again.

"You're lucky. I drank my fill a short while ago. So you can live a few hours longer."

When he turned her loose, she flopped back against the wall, her whole body shaking uncontrollably.

He pulled up a stool from the opposite corner and sat down beside her bench. "I see I have your attention. And your fear. I can feel it wafting off you. Very nice. If you're afraid of me, you should be afraid of Nicholas Vickers, too. I saved his life. I treated him like a son, and look how he betrayed me." He paused before delivering what he must have thought would be his most devastating line. "I'm sure he didn't tell you that he's a vampire, as well."

Mustering what courage she had left, Emma glared at him. "Actually, he did."

Caldwell's eyes narrowed. "I don't believe you."

"Believe what you want."

He stood over her, and she forced herself to remain still. She was *not* going to give him the satisfaction of seeing how truly terrified she was. But when he again took her chin firmly in his hand, she couldn't prevent him from feeling the involuntary trembling of her body.

He tipped back her head again and examined her neck. His thumb stroked her flesh, sending a shiver through her. "Right here. He drank from you. I can see the healed wound. A vampire's saliva has wonderful restorative properties, don't you know? But he definitely sank his teeth into you. More than once, I see."

More than once? But no…unless…

Emma remembered how dazed she'd felt after Nick had taken her blood when he'd been shot—how she'd had no memory of it having happened, just a foggy sense that *something* had transpired.

The same foggy sense she'd had at least a couple other times since she'd been with him.

*Damn him!*

She wasn't about to let Caldwell know how angry and betrayed she felt, though.

"What does that matter?" she said flatly. "He didn't hurt me. You may both be vampires, but he's nothing like you. You control and hurt and *kill* people. He helps them. You're evil. He's good. It's that simple."

Caldwell cocked one eyebrow in a disdainful look. "A very nice speech. But look where goodness has gotten him. He's going to die today—very soon, in fact. Nicholas can't tolerate sunlight as I can. And we wouldn't want him to burn up before he sees *you* die."

He turned abruptly and walked toward the door, but before he exited the cell, he swung toward her again. The look in his eyes made her skin crawl.

"Oh, and one more thing. Don't expect to see sympathy or concern from him as he watches you die. I've convinced him that I sent you to gain his confidence and bring him here. He thinks you betrayed him. A nice irony, don't you think? I get to drain your blood, then tell him I lied about you. And finally I get to rid myself of the enemy who's been stalking me for over a hundred years."

He gave her a considering look. "I'm sorry you're in such an uncomfortable position, but it can't be helped. I want to make sure you'll still be here when I get back."

Emma waited until he had shut the door before she allowed herself to sag against the wall. A film of tears blurred her vision, then welled over and began running down her cheeks. But with her hands chained behind her, she couldn't even wipe them away.

"Nick," she whispered, then pressed her lips together. Caldwell might be listening, and she didn't want him to know the depths of her torment.

Behind her, she squeezed her hands into fists. What a naive little twit she'd been. She had come to Nick's house and hounded him unmercifully until he'd agreed to help her rescue Margaret. Then when she'd seen his bloody shirt and figured out he was a vampire, what had she done? Run away and come tearing down here to…to do what? Persuade Alex Shane to help her, even when she knew it was against his best interests?

She'd made a mess of everything. And this time, no one was going to come to her rescue.

"I'm sorry, Nick," she whispered, not caring anymore who heard her.

As she huddled in her cell, she thought about what she'd said to Caldwell—that he was evil and Nick was good. It was the truth.

And it had nothing to do with either of them being vampires. Their fundamental natures were opposite. And that would be true even if they were both mortal men.

She dragged in a shaky breath and let it out in a rush. All her adult life she'd avoided serious relationships, afraid of repeating her mother's mistakes. She'd dated casually, choosing men who wanted to have a good time but who weren't interested in a long-term commitment. And each time, she'd said goodbye with a carefree wave, all the while feeling unsatisfied and unfulfilled and…lonely.

In the few short days with Nick, she'd been more satisfied and fulfilled than she'd ever been in her life. And she hadn't felt lonely once. But then, he wasn't like any man she had ever known, or any she'd have chosen. And the difference wasn't merely that he was a vampire.

He was solid, steadfast, a man who honored his commitments and kept his word. Really, in her heart of hearts, she knew he was the man she had been looking for all her life. She had known it from the first night she'd dreamed about him.

The night she had fallen in love with him.

In love with a vampire…

Still, she shrank from the very idea. She simply couldn't get past the certain knowledge that Nick—or the vampire in Nick—had betrayed her trust.

He had drunk her blood. Worse, he'd done it without asking or telling her or even allowing her to know he was doing it. She was sure he had used his mental powers to cloud her mind so she wouldn't know what he'd done. He had done it the night in Baltimore, after the police had left. And he had done it at least a couple other times, she was sure.

She squeezed her eyes closed, remembering the night in his bedroom, after she'd triggered his basement alarm. He'd given her a shattering climax, so shattering that she had thought she must have passed out afterward. But she hadn't passed out. He'd zapped her brain so he could satisfy his own need to drink from her without her knowing. She was as certain of it as she was certain that he *hadn't* done it when they'd made love after the debacle in Baltimore. The details of that memory were vivid in her mind—including that it hadn't been as glorious for him as it had been for her. When she'd asked him what was wrong, he had told her that everything was fine.

But it hadn't been fine. He'd denied himself what for him was the ultimate pleasure because...

*Because he cares about you.*

She cared about him, too—deeply. And as she searched her heart, she acknowledged that she could forgive him the night in Baltimore, for taking from her what he had needed to survive.

And she could forgive him the other time, or times, as well.

What she had difficulty forgiving was that he had deprived her of knowing what he was doing. He'd taken away her memories, leaving gaping holes, as if the past few days were a badly edited movie clip that had been broken and stuck back together, with pieces of the critical action missing.

She could understand why he'd done it—to keep from scaring her away. But she couldn't live like that, never knowing when he might decide he knew best what she should and shouldn't remember. She couldn't live with pieces of her life missing, lost to her forever.

But then, she wouldn't have to live like that. In a little while, Caldwell would kill her. Then he would kill Nick.

She clenched her fists, struggling not to break down, because she would go to her death with dignity. She wouldn't give Caldwell the satisfaction of anything else. Yet so many conflicting emotions tore at her. What Nick had done to her was bad enough, but in the depths of her soul, she knew that her own role was far worse.

She bowed her head, her heart breaking, unable to bear the knowledge that the man she loved had lived for more than a hundred and fifty years—and she had brought him here to die.

## *Chapter Fourteen*

Nick turned his head toward the French doors. They were covered with blackout drapes. But dawn would come in a few hours, and then his life would be over.

In a way, that would be a relief.

He had let himself get emotionally involved with Emma. And she had been lying to him all along.

That hurt more than he'd like to admit.

Yet he couldn't quite believe it.

As his mind went over and over the details of the video, he felt sudden hope.

He fought to keep the relief off of his face in case Caldwell—or, more likely, one of his guards—was monitoring the office surveillance camera. Slumping in the chair to which he was still chained, he did his best to present the picture of defeat.

It wasn't easy. Because he'd figured out the truth. Emma had never made love with the

Master. If she had, Caldwell would have taken her blood—he wouldn't have denied himself that pleasure. And Nick knew as surely as he knew the sun would soon rise that there had been no puncture wounds on Emma's neck when he had bitten her for the first time.

It was the sort of thing a male vampire noticed—rather like a mortal man noticed when he entered a woman's body and discovered she was a virgin. It couldn't be faked, either. The vampire's puncture wounds, even if sealed with his saliva, would be visible to another vampire.

No, Caldwell had never had his teeth in Emma's lovely, sweet neck. The woman in the tape had been her sister, Margaret, as he'd thought in the first place.

Nor had the Master had anything to do with the dreams, Nick realized, now that he thought about it. Caldwell had been eager to taunt him with every piece of evidence, real or manufactured, to convince him that Emma had betrayed him. If the dreams he and Emma had shared were part of the trap, Caldwell surely would have mentioned them himself, if only as further proof of his brilliance and power.

No, the dreams had been his and Emma's alone, and their real-world lovemaking had been true and heartfelt. She cared about him—perhaps even loved him as much as he loved her. At the moment, it didn't matter that it couldn't last, that there was no hope of them having any kind of long-term relationship. All that mattered was that the intimacy they had shared had been genuine— and that he loved her.

Nick looked toward the doors again. Dawn wasn't far away. And by then, he and Emma would be dead.

Unless he did something about it—fast.

With his night-tuned vision, Nick scanned the room and located two hidden cameras in opposite corners, near the ceiling. They'd be equipped with night-vision lenses, so the dark wouldn't hide his actions. When he made his move, he would have to be swift and decisive.

Careful to maintain his defeated posture, he closed his eyes and made a fast assessment of his mental and physical condition. Without the anguish of believing that Emma had betrayed him, he quickly realized that he was in better shape than he'd thought. The debilitating effects of Caldwell's mind burst had faded. His mental energy was nearly at full strength.

He directed that energy inward, gathering his strength, focusing on the cells of his arms and legs, pumping up his muscles in preparation for the first task he must perform: getting out of this damn chair.

A KEY RATTLED in the lock of the cell door, and Emma tensed. This was it. They were coming to get her, and she wasn't ready to die.

The guards would have to unfasten her from the ring in the wall, but she didn't see how she could fight her way past them. Still, she had nothing to lose in trying. And, it occurred to her, the guards wouldn't kill her. Caldwell wanted to do that himself.

Her heart pounded, and she held her breath, anticipating the confrontation. She ordered herself to relax. She didn't want to give anything away to Caldwell's goons. Her life depended on convincing them that her spirit was too broken for her to resist.

She let her head fall forward to her chest, hoping she appeared the very epitome of abject defeat. When she heard the door open, her breath froze in her lungs.

But nothing happened—no footsteps, no zombified goons hauling her to her feet. For long seconds she waited. When she couldn't stand the tension another moment, she raised her head— and gasped.

NICK FOCUSED ON the two chain links binding the manacles around his wrists. Sweat broke out on his forehead and his head throbbed as he attempted to tear apart the forged steel. It wasn't working.

Unwilling to give up, he gathered his mental energy and tried again. His whole body grew damp, and pain surged in his head until he thought it would burst. But he felt the links give. Just a bit.

Again he tried…and again. His breath was coming in gasps and his clothing was stuck to his skin, drenched in sweat. And still he remained locked to the chair.

Stifling a groan, he went at it one more time. He had to get free. He was *not* going to allow Damien Caldwell to tie Emma to a stake and drain her blood. He was *not* going to let that bastard bare her lovely body to a crowd of leering men while he touched and stroked her and, finally, sank his fangs into her and—

The chain links moved, the steel turning soft like rubber. Aware of the change, Nick held on to the intolerable image of Caldwell holding Emma's naked and limp body, her blood dripping from his mouth. At the same time, with his muscles bulging, Nick jerked his arms upward.

The chains snapped. He still had the manacles around his wrists, but his arms were no longer bound to the chair.

Quickly, knowing he had only seconds, he bent down and slipped the chain running between his manacled ankles under the chair legs, so that he was completely free of the chair, although his feet were still hobbled.

He stood up at the same instant the door burst open and two men with guns barreled in. Knowing he couldn't risk taking a hit and losing blood before he could rescue Emma, he ducked. Hampered by the leg chains, he threw himself at the man in front, knocking him backward and into his companion.

They both went down, but one of their guns fired. Nick felt a bullet whiz past his ear. With his chains rattling, he stamped his booted foot down on the gun hand of the man who had fired, hearing bone crunch under the blow. The man screamed at the same instant Nick brought his boot down again, this time on the other guard's face, drawing another scream.

Moving fast, he grabbed them both by the hair, hauled them upward and banged their heads together hard enough to knock them both unconscious. Then he fumbled in one of their pockets until he found a small key ring. One of the keys on it opened the locks on his wrist and ankle cuffs.

Freed of all restraint, he started for the door, then stopped. In the hallway, heavy footsteps raced toward the office—drawn by the gunshot or screams or both, he figured.

Nick didn't wait to see who was coming. He sprang to the French doors, kicked them open and, without looking back, leaped into the pre-dawn night. He ducked low and at vampire speed made for a stand of trees fifty feet away.

Although it was still fully dark outside, he could smell the coming dawn. He had to hurry. Based on his previous reconnoiters of the grounds, he had a good idea of where to find Emma. One of the buildings near the woods that Caldwell had outfitted as a prison.

Moving swiftly through patches of woods and even faster across open lawns, he took only a minute or so to get there. But when he threw open the door, his heart skipped a beat, then lurched into heavy pounding inside his chest.

The room was empty. They had already taken Emma to the outdoor amphitheater, where he knew Caldwell held his ceremonies.

Nick hadn't prayed in decades, but as he ran through the night, he chanted silently, "Please, God, please…don't let her be dead. Don't let it happen. Please…"

As he approached the killing ground, he slowed to a walk. No matter how scared he was that he might be too late, he couldn't go rushing in without some kind of plan. Creeping slowly from tree to tree, he arrived at the top of the sunken theater.

Caldwell considered it his sacred ground. Sacred to the devil, maybe.

The place held seating for perhaps fifty people, arranged on tiers around a central stage. Only about half the seats were filled. Of course, the men in those seats were Caldwell's most trusted followers.

In the center of the large square stage was an upright post with a spotlight shining on it. As Nick watched, two men led Emma onto the platform. She was barefoot and dressed in white, and her blond hair was tied at the back of her neck. She walked between them with her head held high, not struggling at all.

Meeting her fate with courage, Nick thought, his heart breaking at the thought of what her outward appearance of calm dignity must be costing her.

With some vague idea of swooping down, scooping her up and flying out of there before Caldwell arrived, Nick took a step away from the shelter of the trees, preparing himself for a single, all-out assault.

A hand clamped onto his arm, stopping him. He whipped around, fist raised in expectation of smashing a guard's face, and he nearly did it before he saw who it was.

"Emma?" he croaked, hardly daring to believe it. "But you're…"

"No," she whispered. "That's Margaret down there."

Casting a quick look around to make sure they hadn't been noticed, he grabbed her hand and pulled her back into the shadows of the trees. When he hauled her into his arms and hugged her, she hugged him back, as if she meant it.

"How did you get away?" he whispered into her hair.

"Margaret," she replied. "She came to my cell to tell me that Caldwell was going to punish me for running away. I tried to tell her what the punishment would be, but she doesn't believe he would kill me, or anybody else. To prove it, she insisted on changing places with me—and I let her, hoping I'd be able to find you or, if all else failed, at least try to get her out of here myself."

"You won't have to," he said. "I will."

They were speaking in whispers, but that didn't detract from the vehemence of her tone as she insisted, "You certainly will not. We'll do it together, exactly as we planned."

"Emma, we don't have the laser anymore, and—"

"Wait." Reaching inside her pants, she pulled out the weapon he'd designed.

He stared at it in disbelief. "How did you manage—"

"A really stupid guard. Never mind the details."

"My darling Emma, you are truly amazing."

The sound of clapping cut his protest short. He and Emma both moved so they had a view of the amphitheater stage without being seen.

Caldwell had stepped onto the stage, dressed in black tights topped by a black, thigh-length tunic. Ignoring Margaret, who was tied to the post, he walked with solemn steps to the front of the platform and began to address his followers.

"I want to thank you for attending this special night," the Master said, spreading his arms wide to embrace his rapt audience. "The woman you see before you insinuated herself into our community like a worm into a living body. She is a false disciple who was never meant to live among us. She fled our household and has only returned because she thought she could destroy all that we have come to hold dear."

Behind him, Margaret whimpered, "No, that's not true. You don't understand."

But Caldwell wasn't listening. He went on ignoring her as he delivered his message to the faithful.

Nick looked around at the eager expressions of the men in the crowd. They were revved up, ready for the show they knew the Master was about to give them. And in their heightened state, they were especially dangerous.

Caldwell was at the end of his speech, and Nick

knew what came next. They hadn't much time. Taking Emma's hand and tugging her a few steps back into the trees, he said, "I'm going to rush him. You stay up here, and when I've killed him, you free Margaret and get out."

"Nick, no!" she whispered, urgency coloring her tone. "Caldwell can't do to my mind what he does to yours."

He gave his head a quick shake. "He caught me off guard, but he won't be able to lay me out again. I'll—"

"No! Nick, please! I dragged you into this mess, and I feel horrible enough about it as it is. To have any chance at all of getting out of it alive, we can't risk having Caldwell zap you again. I need you to be yourself." Her fingers wrapped around his forearms and squeezed. "Please."

He saw the pleading look in her wide, blue gaze. "All right," he sighed, thinking that if he survived the next few minutes and Emma didn't, he might as well let the rising sun obliterate him.

"Good," she said. "So how are we going to do it? You said you'd create a distraction. Where?"

"I wasn't thinking we'd be doing this in front of fifty or sixty of Caldwell's inner circle."

"I know, but that's how it is."

Moving silently, he crept to the top of the theater and looked down at the stage, trying to calculate their best chance.

"This woman has sealed her own fate," Caldwell was saying. "She must pay for the crimes she has committed against us."

Nick hated the entire plan. But he couldn't deny that he and Emma stood a better chance of success together than either of them did alone.

Reluctantly, he thought for a moment, then began speaking rapidly. "When Caldwell shuts up, he'll approach Margaret from behind. He'll spend a few minutes making a show of touching her and playing at lovemaking to give the audience a little sexual thrill. Then he'll bend down to put his mouth against her neck—probably the left side."

Emma stared at him. "You've seen him do this?"

"Yes," Nick replied flatly, then went on with the instructions. "While he's doing his act, you slip around to the other side of the theater. It's dark in back of the spotlight, and everybody will be focused on him. I'll stay on this side of the stage and stand at the top of the stairs. I can see beyond the spotlight, so I'll know when you're in position and I'll make sure nobody is looking your way while you're going down the stairs to get up behind Caldwell."

He heard her draw a ragged little breath. "Okay."

"Use the gun on him the way you saw me use

it on the water," he continued. "Press the button, and the beam will come out the end. But, Emma, you have to get within ten feet of him to do significant damage. Past that, the energy is too diffuse."

She nodded. "I understand."

He took her by the shoulders, squeezing gently. "Ready?"

She nodded again, and he heard the steel in her voice as she said, "Yes, let's do it."

Their gazes met and held, the moment stretching between them.

Then, afraid he might never see her again, unable to speak the words he wanted to say to her, Nick wrapped his hand around the back of her head, pulled her roughly to him and kissed her hard. It was a brief, frantic joining of their mouths, and in it he tasted warmth and compassion and forgiveness. It was all he needed—and more.

He let her go, knowing that if he lived another hundred and fifty years, he'd never find a woman he loved more than he loved Emma.

And a whole lot of good it would do him.

EMMA MADE HER WAY around the top of the theater, heart pounding, senses tuned to every sound from the pitch-black woods, as well as from the stage below.

"It is time," she heard Caldwell say. "In this place, you will hearken to my power. But when you leave this theater, you will not remember what happened here. Now, repeat my order."

As one, a chorus of male voices intoned, "We will not remember."

Emma stifled a sound of disgust. So that's why nobody talked about what happened in this place. They didn't remember.

The Master went through the drill once more, ordering them to forget and securing their agreement. Then he turned from the audience and approached Margaret.

Margaret shrank from him, twisting against the ropes that bound her to the stake. "No, Master, please—" Her voice broke off, and she went suddenly, totally still. Emma realized Caldwell had zapped her into submission.

Stepping up to Margaret, he raised his hands to her head and stroked downward, over her shoulders. Emma expected him to do exactly as Nick had described—put on an X-rated display for the benefit of all the horny goons watching him. Instead, she saw him bend over, lowering his head toward her sister's neck.

*No, wait, I'm not ready!* She hadn't yet arrived in position, dead-center with the back of the stage.

She hurried, hoping her haste didn't cause

noise that would draw attention, wondering how long exactly it took a vampire to drain a body of blood to the point of death.

She didn't have to find out.

"Wait, you're not— That bitch! Where is she?"

Caldwell's angry voice rose like a war cry from the stage. A half second later, Emma ran out of the cover of the woods to the edge of the theater. And a half second after that, she looked across at the top of the stairs opposite her position and saw Nick grab one of the torches that marked the entrance to the arena.

With a bloodcurdling shout, he tossed it into the air so that it sailed into the audience. A man's shirt caught on fire, and he began to scream. Nick grabbed the other torch and waved it over his head.

"Who's next?" he bellowed.

"Get him!" Caldwell shouted.

Some of the men jumped to their feet and rushed up the stairs. Others remained where they were, seemingly stunned.

Nick gave the first of the attackers who reached him an almighty shove, sending him into the men coming up behind him. They fell like dominoes—two, three, four of them—before one managed to remain on his feet.

Emma didn't waste time. Quickly, laser gun in hand, she crept down the dark slope of the theater toward Caldwell and her sister. The Master had his back toward her, watching the action at the top of the stairs. A crowd of men were converging on Nick, and she had to fight off all her fears for his safety, as well as an overwhelming desire to run like hell in the other direction. The only way to end this was to remove the man who was directing the action.

Margaret made a moaning sound, and Emma was pleased to see her fighting hard against the ropes that bound her. Had she finally realized how wrong she'd been about Caldwell? Did she now believe he would have killed her with no more remorse than if he'd kicked a dog?

Emma reached the bottom of the slope and pulled herself up onto the shoulder-height wooden stage. But she still had at least twenty-five feet to go before she'd be within firing range of Caldwell. She started to creep silently toward him when, abruptly, as if he knew someone was behind him, he turned.

"Who dares…?" He trailed off, having spotted her. "How the hell did you get out?" he shouted.

"I let her out," Margaret cried plaintively, "to prove you weren't going to hurt her."

"Your mistake. I'm going to kill you, you bitch. But first I'm going to kill your sister."

With a snarl, he charged Emma.

It took every scrap of courage she had to wait

for him to get close enough. Twenty feet…her whole body trembled…fifteen feet…her clammy-cold hand gripped the laser at her side…ten feet.

She raised the gun into firing position, aiming directly for Caldwell's black heart, and pushed the button. A beam of red light shot out of the front end and struck Caldwell squarely on target.

Stumbling to a halt, he made a strangled sound. "Down here! Come get this bitch," he bellowed to his followers as he tried to dodge the beam.

Most of the men were engaged with Nick, but from the corner of her eye she saw a small army turn around and start toward her.

Margaret struggled desperately with her bonds and finally wrenched herself free.

"No!" she shouted, launching herself at Emma.

Emma cried out as her sister imposed her body between the gun and the target. Frantically, she snapped off the light beam. "Down! For God's sake, Marg, get *down!*"

Margaret kept coming. "Stop! Don't kill him, please!" she gasped.

Emma's only option was to grab her sister and fling her off the back edge of the stage.

Caldwell was right behind her, staggering but still erect. Knowing she had only seconds, Emma aimed and fired again, and again hit the Master directly in the chest.

He screamed, but kept coming.

Desperate, Emma tried to sidestep, her aim going a bit wild as she cast quick glances over her shoulder to see where she was going. But all she accomplished was to back herself into the corner of the stage, where her choice was to fall off, allowing Caldwell to jump down on her and finish her, or to stand firm.

He reached her before she had a chance to make a decision, snatching a handful of her hair and twisting it to hold her. Still, she kept her finger firmly on the laser's firing mechanism.

The Master gave her hair a terrible yank. Then, suddenly, he let go. Roaring in anger, he whirled to face the other direction, throwing his arm in front of his head as though to ward off a blow. "Nicholas! Damn you!" he screamed. "Get out of my head!"

Shooting a quick look at the top of the stairs, Emma saw only a horde of Caldwell's followers engaged in a brawl. It was impossible to tell if Nick was under the melee. Regardless, she was sure he had attacked Caldwell in the same vampiric way that Caldwell had attacked him earlier.

Nick's mental blast wasn't strong enough to kill the Master, but it gave her the time she needed to do what had to be done.

She fired at Caldwell's back, and when he spun to face her again, she hit him in the same spot as before, over his heart, where the hole in his clothing exposed pale but singed flesh. Caldwell made a grab for the weapon and managed to get his hand around it, over hers.

Still she kept the gun in her grasp and her finger on the trigger. In another few seconds, she felt Caldwell's fingers slide forward until he was grasping only the barrel of the gun. Then they slid off of that, too.

A large hole had opened in his chest. With a terrible gurgling sound, he sank to his knees.

"No. By all the saints, *no-oo,*" he screamed, his voice ending in a wail of agony.

He clawed at his chest as though he could dig out the pain. Then he pitched forward, his scream fading to an anguished moan, then…nothing.

He lay absolutely still, a pool of blood spreading out around him. He was dead.

For several seconds a wall of silence held the crowd below the stage at bay. Emma, too, was immobilized by what she'd done, her gaze riveted to the dead vampire lying in front of her.

Then somebody shouted, "Bitch! What have you done?" The angry cry released the men who had been too paralyzed to attack Nick and had, instead, been watching the drama on the stage. Howling, they rose from their seats as one and rushed toward her, murder in their eyes.

# Chapter Fifteen

Emma had nowhere to go. She was backed into a corner of the stage, and her instinct was to jump down and start running up the slope, toward the woods. But she knew she'd never make it even to the trees before they caught her.

"Stay back!" she cried, raising the weapon she had used on Caldwell. "I don't want to hurt you, but I will!"

They kept coming, piling up the steps at the front of the stage, plowing across it toward her.

She hesitated briefly. It had been easy to justify wiping Caldwell from the face of the earth, but she couldn't kill men who had been under his mental control and who undoubtedly were still acting on his orders.

Pointing the laser weapon at the stage, she seared a line in the boards. Smoke rising from the charred wood brought the raging horde to a stumbling halt.

"This gun will do the same thing to you!" she shouted.

Clearly unsure of what to do, they paced and turned and bumped into each other, hurling curses. Then someone among them gasped and pointed to Caldwell.

Emma's gaze followed the man's outstretched arm, and she stared in horror at the thing that lay sprawled on the stage. As they watched, his flesh was melting off his bones.

"Look!" she yelled. "See what he really is."

A sound of dismay went up from the crowd.

"What the hell?" somebody shouted.

"Yes, hell!" Emma agreed. "That's where he's going."

The exposed flesh on Caldwell's body was completely gone now, and the bones were beginning to melt. The skull collapsed, and beneath the black tights and tunic, the skeleton shriveled and shrank away. Finally there was nothing left but a heap of black cloth.

Some of the men sank to their knees and began to wail in grief. Others stood shivering in fear.

"Take a good look," Emma said to them, her voice loud and strong despite her own trembling. "Do you know why he's disappeared like that? He wasn't human! He was a vampire! A centuries-old vampire!"

Stunned silence greeted her announcement.

"A what?" someone whispered.

"A vampire," she repeated. "And now he's turned to dust."

"No!" another man shouted. "It can't be! It's a trick!"

"What more evidence do you want? Or is he still messing with your heads, even in death? He tricked you into staying here to be his food." Emma paused, trying to gauge the men's reactions. Tempering her tone, she added, "He's gone now, and you can go back to being yourselves. You're safe."

But as her gaze scanned the crowd, taking in their expressions, she wasn't certain at all that *she* was safe. It appeared to her that they were plotting their revenge.

Gripping the laser gun, she looked at the fight still raging at the top of the amphitheater. Where in God's name was Nick?

NICK FOUGHT FOR HIS LIFE, beating off one after the other of the men assaulting him. He threw some back, slamming them into the mob that kept coming, but they simply trampled over their fallen comrades in their drive to get to him.

His stamina was waning. Breaking out of his shackles, flying across acres of the estate to find Emma, hurling the bolt of energy into Caldwell's mind—all of it had weakened him, and he had been barely recovered from the Master's earlier mental blow.

As he tried to fend off the angry mob, he felt another threat creeping relentlessly toward him: the sun. It was about to burst over the horizon. If he couldn't extricate himself from the melee before then, he'd be finished.

But he couldn't go anywhere until he was sure Emma was safe. Where was she? Had she killed Caldwell? Or had the Master overcome her?

The fear that she was still in mortal danger kept him fighting for his own life, defending himself in a desperate effort to break free of the mob and get to her.

Dimly, from far away, he heard a whirring sound that he couldn't immediately identify with the enraged attackers swarming over him. They fought like madmen, punching, kicking, doing damage any way they could. His ribs cracked. His nose broke. His kidneys screamed in agony. Still, he fought on, praying he could get to Emma.

In the darkness, a shot rang out. Then another.

The crowd of men beating on him went still for an instant, then began to scatter.

Dazed, Nick staggered on his feet.

"You look like crap."

The vaguely familiar voice, coming from his right, brought him around to see Alex Shane striding toward him.

"I'll be…okay," Nick insisted. "Emma…"

"She's fine," Alex said. "She held the mob off with…what the hell was that thing, anyway? Looked like a damned flashlight."

"A laser gun. I didn't have time to refine the design."

"She singed their toes with it."

Light footsteps clattered on the steps. Turning, he saw Emma rushing toward him.

She stopped five feet away and gasped. "Oh, Lord…*Nick!*"

"I'll be fine." Swaying on his feet, he turned his gaze toward the horizon. "But the sun…"

"Yes, I know."

"Bring a stretcher," Alex shouted.

"I can walk." Nick turned and began limping toward the house. Two men with a stretcher caught up with him.

"You won't make it in time," Emma said gently, walking at his side. "Lie down."

He did it for her, and as soon as he got horizontal, he wondered how he had managed to stay on his feet.

"He's allergic to the sun," she said, speaking to Alex and the other unfamiliar men. "Get him inside. Fast."

It was too late. The first rays shot over the horizon, and Nick felt needles of pain digging into his skin. It was worse than the injuries from the fight. The men carrying the stretcher began to run.

"The office," he said, his voice so weak that he could barely hear it above the roaring in his ears. "Blackout...shades."

"Right," Emma said, keeping pace with the stretcher bearers. "This way," she told them.

He felt the difference the moment they passed through the French doors of the office, and in the next instant, someone pulled the blinds and the needles stopped stabbing into his flesh. Still, he was losing consciousness fast. The stretcher, it seemed, had legs, and he felt the jerk and heard the clicks as they were pulled down and locked into place, forming a bed.

He heard voices murmuring about the chains he'd left lying on the floor, with their broken, twisted links. When someone else mentioned a doctor, he tried to speak, tried to stop them.

Emma's voice cut in. "He'll heal if you just leave him be."

Another voice sounded doubtful, but his brave and determined Emma insisted that they leave him alone, that he would be all right.

Confident that she would win the argument, he almost smiled. He was safe. Emma wouldn't let anyone hurt him.

And with that last thought, he sank into unconsciousness.

WHEN NICK AWOKE, he was alone in the room. Cautiously, he took a physical inventory. Some of his bones had been broken but were already almost whole again. He'd had some other internal damage, but it seemed to be taking care of itself. When he sat up, the pain in his gut was only a dull ache.

And he was powerfully hungry. Moving as fast as he could, he crossed the Oriental carpet to the private bathroom attached to the office. He leaned over the sink, peering into the mirror to inspect the damage to his face—some bruising, a new bump in his previously broken nose. Nothing serious.

The torn and filthy clothing was another matter. He didn't fancy facing Emma and whoever else was here looking like a war refugee.

He soon discovered that someone had already anticipated his need. A shirt and a pair of jeans lay neatly folded on the desk. Likewise, new toiletries awaited on the vanity in the bathroom.

Nick stood for a long time under a hot shower, letting the water pound on his body. It felt heavenly. After he dried off, he brushed his teeth and combed his hair. He didn't have to shave. His beard grew so slowly that he could take care of it every month or so.

As he dressed, he felt his jaw clench. Even though he looked a hell of a lot better, he didn't want to face Emma. Or Alex Shane, or the other men who were doubtless also from Shane's agency.

He had a more urgent problem, though. His mouth was so dry that his tongue was sticking to the roof of his mouth. He needed to drink.

He walked to the French doors, thinking he would slake his thirst first, then decide what to do about Emma and the rest of them—which might be to swim across the river and go home.

Home. His time there was up. He'd come too close to exposure by the events of the past week. Too many people had seen things that might lead to dangerous conclusions about him. He would have to pull out the new identity that he'd readied and find another place to settle. He had known all along that he would eventually have to leave his rural Maryland lair. But dammit, he wasn't ready.

He pushed aside the drapes, then opened the French doors and stepped onto the patio, sending his mind before him, searching for the deer he knew must be in the vicinity. When he found a doe, he soothed her with his thoughts.

"It's all right," he crooned. "It won't hurt. And you'll like it."

She accepted his presence easily, and he slung his arm over her back, stroking her stiff fur.

"You're a beauty," he whispered. "I'll take a

little of your blood. Not much. Just enough to feed me tonight."

Then he bent his head and sank his fangs into her neck, feeling the surge of heat and life as blood poured into his mouth. He took what he needed, then released her.

"Go join your companions."

She rubbed her head against his hand as though she understood, then took off into the woods.

When he turned to head back to the house, he saw Emma standing a few feet away, watching him. His heart stopped, then started pounding.

"How long have you been there?" he asked.

"Long enough."

"And now you're disgusted," he concluded.

"Actually, no."

He gave her a skeptical look.

She shrugged. "Deer are a good solution to your problem. You could be killing people the way Caldwell did. But you never kill, do you?"

"Not anymore. I did, a long time ago." Because he felt weak in the knees, he walked to the nearest tree and propped his shoulders against the trunk.

She eyed him speculatively before observing, "You mean, before you got out from under the Master's thrall and learned you could control your urges."

"Yes."

She turned, wandering a few steps to look

toward the river. "Those books…" she began. "The ones about vampires that you said were in your library. Would you…would you mind if I read some?"

Yeah, he'd mind.

"Sure," he said. "Go ahead. But why?"

"Well…I thought they might help me understand you," she said, strolling toward him.

He stiffened, pushing away from the tree trunk to stand rigidly upright.

Taking note of his posture, Emma stopped a few paces away. "I can see you aren't ready to handle a personal discussion. So let's start with easy stuff. Well, not exactly easy, but not directed at you."

"What are you talking about?" he asked.

"While you were sleeping, Alex Shane and his friends from the Light Street Detective Agency started working with Caldwell's followers," she explained. "Turns out, some of them were here because they were too afraid of Caldwell to leave. That includes Anabel Lewis, the woman Alex was looking for. Those people have all gone home. Some others left because they were afraid they'd be arrested."

Nick frowned. "Shouldn't some of them—guards, mostly—have been turned over to the cops?"

"Maybe. But they cleared out in the confusion after Caldwell disappeared."

"Disappeared? So the laser worked."

She hitched in a breath, then let it out. "Yes. Technically, I killed him, but his body just turned to ashes that have all scattered. So there's nothing for the cops to find."

"Witnesses?" he suggested.

Emma smiled. "It seems that nobody who saw what happened remembers any of it."

Nick's frown turned thoughtful for a moment. Then comprehension dawned. "Caldwell," he said. "He ordered them to forget."

She nodded. "A case of mass hypnosis. Apparently, although the Master liked to put on shows— or show off, I guess—for his inner circle, he obviously did it entirely for his own pleasure. His viewers were deprived of the memories, so they couldn't rat on him. And, fortunately—" she smiled "—the same applies to me. Nobody remembers anything at all that happened in the amphitheater, including my killing Caldwell. They just know he's disappeared, which makes a lot of them seriously upset and confused. The Light Street Foundation—that's another agency in the same building as Alex's Baltimore office—has several psychologists and social workers on tap. A bunch of them have been counseling Caldwell's ex-followers—the ones still here, anyway, which I figure is about a third. One of the psychologists, Kathryn Kelley, thinks most of the people will be ready to go home by the end of the week. The really disturbed ones, like Margaret, will get more help."

Emma's gaze dropped to her fingers, toying with the button of her blouse just above the waistband of her slacks.

"She'll be okay," Nick said gently, and he hoped it was true. Tipping his head to the side, he lightened his tone. "Sounds like a hell of a lot got accomplished in one day."

Emma's lips quirked upward. "Sorry to shock you, but you slept for two days."

"Good Lord. I've never done that before."

"I guess your body needed the extra time after two ordeals in a row."

He didn't want to talk about himself. He didn't want to talk at all. He wanted to pull her into his arms and...

"I saw the video," she said, casting him a glance from under lowered lashes. "The one where Caldwell has me agree to go after you."

"It wasn't you," he said. "It was Margaret."

"You know that for certain? When he showed it to you, you didn't think it might be me?"

"Well..." He waited until she had raised her gaze to his. "Maybe he had me fooled for a few minutes."

"What changed your mind?"

"Caldwell asked if you wanted to make love

with him *again.* I knew you'd never made love with him even once, so the woman in the tape had to be your twin."

A puzzled frown flickered over her brow. "How did you know I hadn't made love with him?"

"Because he would have taken your blood, and there were no bite marks on your neck before... before the first time I drank from you."

"So..." She drew a shaky little breath. "You admit you bit me more than once."

He waited, not denying the charge.

"And now," she added, "you're thinking I might walk away from you."

"That certainly would be the wisest choice."

He'd surprised her. He saw it in the brief widening of her lovely blue eyes.

"What if I don't want to?" she said, a note of challenge in her voice. "What if I want to stick around?"

He cocked one eyebrow. "Stick around with a vampire?"

"You're not like Caldwell."

"No, I'm not. But, Emma—" he heaved a sigh "—the late, unlamented Master and I do have a few fundamental things in common by virtue of our both being vampires. One of them is that making love to me means drawing blood." He shook his head sadly. "You found out what happened when I did that twice in a couple of days—the first time, when you came to my bedroom after setting off the alarm and the second, after we'd gone back to my house from Baltimore. You got sick and dizzy. It doesn't take much of that for a woman to become anemic."

She gave a small, one-shouldered shrug. "There's always iron pills."

He snorted. "You know that's no long-term solution. Emma, we have to face it that there's no way we can stay together."

"But you made love to me without…drinking."

"And, as you sensed, it wasn't very good for me," he said bluntly. "I climax like a mortal man, but for total fulfillment, I must be connected with the woman through her blood at the moment of climax. Without that…well, suffice it to say it's frustrating, and the frustration grows with repetition."

"So maybe we'd have to…you know, space it out. Not do it so often."

He smiled sadly. "My darling Emma, you know that wouldn't last a week. I can barely stand here looking at you without ripping off our clothes and tumbling you onto some nice soft grass, and—"

"I get the picture," she muttered hurriedly. Then, with a sigh, she admitted, "And you're right. I wouldn't be able to keep my hands off of you, either."

"So you see the problem," he said. "I can't be around you without wanting you. And I can't have you without wanting to drink from you. It's an impossible situation."

"I don't believe in impossible."

He knew that. It was one of the things he loved about her. But he'd lived too long not to know that there were problems to which there truly were no solutions. Theirs was one of them.

Well, nearly so. But he couldn't be the one to suggest the one obvious way they could be together. It would have to come from her, and he had no hope, no hope at all, that she ever would suggest it.

"You're trying to drive me away, aren't you?" she said.

"I'm merely pointing out the reality."

"Well, reality sucks." Turning to face him, she lifted her chin in a defiant look he'd come to recognize. "But we might be able to work it out, if you're willing to try."

"Emma, for God's sake, don't you think I've tried before? There is no way to reconcile our differences—those being that you're a mortal woman, and I'm a vampire."

With a cry of frustration, she threw her hands wide. "Nick, I love you."

It was what he'd wanted to hear. Odd that it should make him so very happy and, at the same time, so very sad.

"And I love you," he said quietly.

"Good!" she snapped. "So doesn't that mean anything to you?"

"It means a great deal. But it doesn't change what I am."

"Right. Fine. You'd rather fly off into the night, like some damned bat from a B-grade horror movie. Run away if you want. But I hope, before you vanish without a trace, you'll come back to the house and talk to Alex and the others. They'd really like to get to know you."

With that, she whirled and stomped off toward the house.

A shiver of panic raced up his spine. "You've been *discussing* me with Shane and his cronies?"

Without missing a step, she tossed a reply over her shoulder. "Find out for yourself!"

## Chapter Sixteen

Nick stayed where he was for a long time. He thought about what life would be like with Emma at his side. He fantasized about taking her places, traveling the world with her, showing her things, some that would thrill the adventurer in her, others that would inspire the artist, and still others that would appeal to her deep-rooted sense of humanity.

But it was just a fantasy. He should go back to his lonely existence. He had survived without Emma before she'd come crashing into his life. He could do it again.

Yet he found it wasn't so easy to…fly off into the night, as she'd put it.

In the end, he followed her footsteps back to the house and spotted Alex Shane through one of the open French doors leading into the dining room. He thought about heading in the other direction, then changed his mind. Maybe he'd find out what

Emma had meant, saying that Shane and his cohorts wanted to get to know him.

When he walked into the dining room, he found the detective sitting with a group of men and women.

Alex looked toward him and smiled. "Nick! How are you feeling?"

"Better. Thanks," he said cautiously.

"Come, join us. I'd like you to meet some of the people I work with."

He introduced Hunter and Kathryn Kelley, Jed Prentiss, Jason Zacharias, Steve Claiborne, Jo O'Malley, Cameron Randolph, Thorn and Cassie Devereaux and Dan and Sabrina Cassidy.

Nick nodded at each as Alex ticked off the names. He got nothing but friendly smiles and looks in return, but he couldn't help wondering what they'd been told about him.

Curiosity driving him, he asked, "What are you all doing here?"

"Mopping up," Alex answered.

"There's a lot of fascinating information in Caldwell's files," the man named Jed Prentiss said.

"I'm sure," Nick murmured, trying not to sound too eager.

Alex cleared his throat. "I know you put a lot of effort into nailing the bastard. You're welcome to review any of the material. We wouldn't have it if you hadn't had the guts to take him on."

Nick shifted his weight from one foot to the other. "Thanks. Uh, yeah, I would like to look at some of the stuff."

"We've put it in the library."

"Thanks," he said again, wondering if he were coming across like an idiot.

Growing more uncomfortable by the second, he backed away. They let him go without comment.

It had been a long time since he'd simply chatted with so many people at once.

He was more comfortable alone in the library, looking through the research materials Caldwell had collected over the years. There were a lot of psychology textbooks, as well as information on hypnosis and mind control. He found books on blood chemistry and a wide variety of other medical subjects—so many that he wondered if Caldwell had actually been worried about getting AIDS or some other blood-borne illness.

The Master had also kept diaries documenting the enclaves where he'd lived and the people who'd lived and died there—with no dates noted, although even the most casual reader could have figured out that the diaries had to span more than a mortal lifetime.

Nick was transfixed by what his longtime enemy had chosen to write down—and just as interested in what he'd left out. As he read the account of what had happened in France, it finally hit him: He had accomplished his goal. He'd killed the demon who'd murdered Jeanette.

He'd expected to feel triumphant. Instead, he simply felt empty.

With a harsh laugh, he wondered if he were about to fall into some kind of identity crisis, having lost his sense of purpose. All these years, he'd felt guilty about Jeanette. Killing Caldwell wiped the slate clean, so to speak. But the elation was missing. Maybe because it had happened so many years ago that all true pain or grief he'd felt had long since dissipated.

But it was more than that. He'd thought Jeanette was the most fascinating woman he'd ever met. He'd since met other women whom he could have loved—but very carefully and deliberately hadn't.

And then he'd met Emma.

His heart squeezed at the very thought of her name. Could it be true that she was right, that they could find a way to be together, if only he would try? Did he dare hope there might be a solution to their problem?

He looked at the books and journal articles lying scattered on the large oak table at which he was sitting. Might the answer lie in one of these books?

It was late, nearly dawn. If the answer was here, he wasn't going to find it tonight.

Rising from his chair, he returned to the office, locked the door, made sure all the blinds were down and flopped onto the wide leather couch. He lay staring at the ceiling, thinking about Emma. About possibilities.

About how he would feel if it turned out the situation wasn't quite as impossible as he had always believed it to be.

NICK SPENT the next few nights reading and, in short intervals, talking with the men and women who worked with Alex Shane. He noted early on that they all acted toward him with almost studied casualness. Nobody pushed him to talk about anything serious. They talked about jobs they'd taken on, and they expressed interest in his own cases. Thorn Devereaux asked enthusiastically about the laser gun and, in exchange for an explanation of its workings, shared information about some of his own rather startling inventions.

Nick wondered why they were all going out of their way to be so friendly, so congenial, so…nice. But he couldn't deny that despite his initial reticence—the result of being out of practice—he was rapidly growing to enjoy the company.

He would have enjoyed Emma's company, too, but he hadn't had so much as a minute of it. She was still at the estate. Sometimes he saw her from a distance. But she never sought him out and always seemed to be where he wasn't. He guessed she'd taken his "Danger—Keep Out" message to heart, and having found nothing in all of Caldwell's literature that might feed his foolish hopes, he knew it was for the best. But it made him heartsick.

Three evenings after he'd woken up from the assault on Caldwell and his minions, he went out to visit the deer herd. When he returned to the mansion, he heard voices in the dining room.

Most of the people he'd already met were grouped around one of the long tables, which was laden with a feast—everything from pastries and muffins to deli meats and salads.

"Sit down and join us," the man named Thorn suggested.

"I'm…not really hungry," he said.

Jed Prentiss spoke with his mouth half-full of potato salad. "I don't know what you've found in Caldwell's diaries, but one thing I discovered were notes on how the bastard was training himself to eat regular food."

Nick stared at him. They hadn't discussed the Master at all. Cautiously, he said, "What do you mean?"

"You know what I mean," Jed replied. "We know what Caldwell was. And before you decide it's high time you got the hell out of here, you might be interested to know that I'm a zombie."

Nick felt his jaw sag but couldn't help it.

"Thorn, here—" Jed nodded toward his colleague "—is a space alien. And Hunter is a clone. But, hell, nobody's perfect. We all seem to get along all right. And, you know, some quirks and idiosyncrasies can come in handy, as I'm sure you've discovered yourself from time to time."

Nick stared at him, and Hunter and Thorn, utterly speechless.

"We're, uh, an unusual group. There's room for a lot of diversity in the Light Street Detective Agency. And we're hoping you'll consider joining us."

Nick's gaze narrowed. "Did Emma tell you what I am?"

Alex shook his head. "Naw, we had it figured out before we got here the other night. After I put you and Emma into that rowboat, I was feeling bad about letting you mount an invasion on your own. So I called Hunter. I already had my suspicions about you, but I didn't know what to make of them."

"The only logical conclusion based on the evidence," Hunter said, "was that you were a vampire."

"Nick, you look like you need to sit down," Jo O'Malley commented.

"Yes, I believe I do." He pulled out a chair and sat, then surveyed the table of friendly faces.

He had been alone for so long, believing he'd never again enjoy the company of others who shared his interests and concerns. Believing that he'd never again be given the opportunity to form true friendships. It never would have occurred to him to go looking for what he had learned not to want or need. But here these people were offering it to him—even knowing what he was. He was overwhelmed.

"You don't have to give us an answer now," Alex said.

"But think about it," Jed added.

"You're *sure* you understand everything about me?" he asked.

Alex gave him a direct look. "We have a very resourceful research department. We did a thorough background investigation on you—and when I say thorough, I mean the report goes back about a hundred and fifty years. Starting around 1858, we know you were capturing slave ships bound for Charleston, South Carolina, and returning the Africans to their homelands. We also know you assisted the Underground Railroad *while* you were running blockades to bring food and medical supplies to the South during the Civil War."

Jo picked up where Alex stopped. "You saved the lives of a lot of miners during the Klondike gold rush. You were a spy for our side in World

War I, and you smuggled Jews out of Nazi Germany during World War II."

"And—" Jed gave him a grin "—we know why you feed the deer who live around your house in Howard County. All the evidence says that you're the kind of guy we'd like to have on our team."

Nick stared at him. "I thought I'd covered my tracks. It's unbelievable that you could have found so much."

"You covered your tracks just fine," Alex said. "But, like I said, we've got superior research skills."

Nick's gaze swung around the room. "Well, now that you mention it, I've done a bit of research, too. I know the kind of assignments your agency takes. I know you've pulled off raids under the noses of a number of police departments. I also know that you specialize in saving the good guys from the bad guys." Looking around the room again, focusing briefly on each expectant face, he took the plunge. "And I know one more thing—that I'd like very much to join you."

"Good!" Jed and Alex both exclaimed.

There were smiles and words of appreciation around the table.

"We can talk about details later," Alex said. "We just wanted you to know that we saw you as an asset."

When the meeting broke up soon after, Nick felt better than he had in a very long time. But there was one important matter that remained unresolved.

He had to talk to Emma.

He'd been through the entire first floor, searching for her, when he ran into Jo O'Malley in the entrance hall.

"Are you looking for Emma?" she asked.

"Yes."

"Come out onto the patio," she said, and they went outside.

Standing square in front of him, Jo looked at him directly. "I'm going to be blunt. You think your problems with Emma are unique, but every relationship has rough patches. A few years ago, I was shot in an ambush and had a near-death experience. I guess God wasn't ready for me to cross over, because I came back to earth. But my deceased husband, Skip O'Malley, followed me back. His ghost hung around, fighting with Cam, who, if you haven't figured it out yet, is my present husband. Well, Skip and Cam never liked each other when Skip was alive, and death didn't improve the situation."

Nick knew he was gawking at her. "You're telling the truth?"

"I don't have enough imagination to make up something as weird as this," she assured him. "And it gets even weirder. A very bad man kidnapped me. He was going to kill me, and the only way Cam could rescue me was to let Skip invade his mind and take over his body."

She was right. It was too weird to be fiction.

"What I'm trying to say is, keep your mind open, and you may be surprised by what happens."

"I will, if I can find Emma."

"She's been keeping to herself, sleeping on the cabin cruiser we brought down from Travis Stone's estate." Jo gestured toward the luxury cruiser moored at the end of the estate's main dock. Then, giving his arm a squeeze, she added, "Good luck."


EMMA SET DOWN the book she'd been reading by the light of a battery-powered lamp.

The tome had the ominous title *Night Terrors,* and it was one of the vampire treatises she'd taken from Nick's library.

As he'd said, some were written by men—and one by a woman—who claimed to be vampires. Now having finished three and skimmed several others, she had come to believe the claims.

She had wanted to understand Nick, but there was so much variation in the accounts of vampiric life that she'd quickly realized each vampire made his or her own choices, as any human would. Some took pleasure in killing people, while others, like Nick, went to great lengths to avoid harming mortals. A few lived in covens with other vampires, but the majority kept to themselves.

From what she'd read, Caldwell had developed more talents than most. There were others who had learned to overcome the rays of the sun, at least for brief periods of time, but even they could stay awake only a few hours during the day.

As she read, Emma had wondered if she could adjust to life with a vampire. Would it be possible to maintain a committed relationship— a marriage—to someone for hundreds and hundreds of years? Lord, her own mother hadn't been able to stick with the same man for more than a few years. What was there to make her think that she could do better?

The answer to that question was Nick. She had known since he'd first walked into her dreams that they were meant to be together. Whether it was fate or lucky chance or a combination of her desperation and his vampiric mental abilities that had first brought them together, surely a bond as strong as the one they had forged would weather a lot of storms, growing, changing, adjusting as needed, but never disappearing.

At that moment, she heard footsteps on the boards of the long dock. Her head snapped up, and she saw a figure coming toward her. She could barely see through the dark, but she knew it was Nick.

Her heart skipped a beat, then leaped to her throat, all her hopes and fears bubbling to the surface.

NICK STOPPED BESIDE the cruiser's aft deck, his hands shoved into his pockets, staring at Emma and thinking how lovely she looked in the moonlight.

"Do you want some company?" he said.

She remained seated in her deck chair, feigning calm. "That depends."

"On what?"

"On whether we're going to have an honest conversation."

"That's a pretty confrontational way to start."

"I'm too tired to fence with you."

"I never did like fencing." Placing a hand on the gunwale, he vaulted onto the cruiser's deck, then stood looking down at her.

She raised her face toward him. "There's something I've been wondering about. You've told me that if we make love, you won't be satisfied unless you take blood from me. But what about Jeanette? Why wasn't that true with her?"

He gave a short laugh. "That's certainly getting right to the point, isn't it?"

"Yes."

"I never had intercourse with Jeanette."

Her brow furrowed. "But I thought—"

"In the first place," he explained, "society's rules were different then. A man didn't sleep with a woman whom he didn't intend to marry unless she was a widow, someone else's wife or a whore. In the second place, Jeanette was eighteen and a virgin. We were together for months before I dared even to kiss her. Then, before there was a chance of things going any further, Caldwell put her under his control, seduced her and killed her."

"I see," Emma murmured. "But what about other women?"

"As much as possible, I've avoided ones I thought I might come to love, for the reasons I already gave you."

She set down the book she'd been reading, and he realized it was one from his library. Standing, she took a step toward him.

"You must have been lonely," she said in a small voice.

Bloody hell, she could be ruthless. "Yes," he grated.

She crossed the space between them, and there was no way he could stop himself from taking her in his arms. And once he had her, he was lost.

He lifted her up and sat down in one of the deck chairs, cradling her on his lap. When her arms tightened around him, he breathed in the delicate flowery scent of her shampoo and the fresh, womanly smell of her skin, and he sighed.

She pressed her forehead against his temple, clinging to him.

"What if we could solve the problem?"

He couldn't help the tension that immediately crept into his body. "How?"

He heard her drag in a breath. Then she let it out in a rush of words. "Are you going to be angry if I tell you I talked to Thorn—in a kind of roundabout way?"

"No," he said, although that wasn't entirely true.

"Thorn was trained as a biologist. He suggested that maybe you only need to take a little of my blood. A very little."

He took her by the shoulders and set her far enough away from himself so that he could look into her eyes. "You'd take the risk of my being able to do that?"

"Yes. I'd do a lot to stay with you. The question is—what are you willing to do for me?"

"What do you mean?" he asked cautiously.

"You took my blood twice. Each time, you clouded my mind. I can't live that way. If we make love, I have to know what's happening."

He swallowed. "I…"

"Are you afraid to do that?" she challenged.

"Yes."

"Why?"

He didn't want to answer but knew he had to. "I'm afraid you'll be repulsed and…frightened of me."

"Perhaps we should put that to the test."

He drew back, studying her face. "You really think you can deal with my drinking from you, knowing it's happening?"

A cold chill skittered over his skin as he tried to imagine what it would be like taking blood from her while she was aware of him doing it. He truly didn't know if he had the nerve to risk it— to risk seeing the look of horror and revulsion on her face. But if he didn't try…

His mouth was so dry he could barely speak. "When would you want to try that?"

"Well, how about now?"

Raising her head, she stroked her lips against his. Just that small contact sent the blood pounding through his veins. She started with that light touch, then deepened the contact, nibbling at his lower lip, then soothing him with her tongue.

He gave the pleasure back to her. Yet some part of him couldn't quite believe in the magic of being with her again.

"Relax," she murmured against his mouth.

"How do you know I'm not?"

"You're as nervous as I am. I can feel it."

Her admission helped.

"But I'm enjoying being with you again. So much," she whispered as she slid her lips to his cheek, then nibbled on his ear.

He raised his hands, stroking his fingers through the silky, moonlit strands of her blond hair. Catching one of his hands, she lowered it to her breast, and he felt her hardened nipple pressing into his palm. His breathing had already grown ragged, and he was as hard as a rock. Yet it was difficult to caress her so intimately, thinking about how she wanted this to end.

"Nick, I want this. Don't hold back on me. Please." Smiling at him, she stood and took his hand, then led him into the main cabin. Standing in the middle of the thick carpet, she began to open the buttons down the front of her blouse.

But he saw that her hands weren't entirely steady. She wasn't quite as sure of herself as she was pretending to be.

"My sweet Emma," he whispered, reaching to help her, their fingers tangled together as they opened the placket.

She was the one who pulled the blouse off and reached to open the catch at the back of her bra. "Take off your shirt," she murmured. "I want to feel your chest against my breasts."

He did as she asked, then gathered her to him, and they both gasped at the sensation of his naked flesh against hers. He was so aroused that he could barely think, but one thing he knew: He must use every skill he possessed to make this good for her.

Easing away, he traced the sweet shape of her breasts with his hands, then bent to swirl his tongue around one pebbled nipple before sucking it into his mouth.

"Oh, Nick," she gasped, reaching to stroke her fingers through his hair, holding him to her.

When she swayed on her feet, he raised his head. "Maybe we should…get horizontal."

"A good idea. Give me a few seconds first." She steadied her hand against his shoulder while she skimmed her slacks and panties down her legs.

He stared at her, thinking she had made herself totally vulnerable to him. To a man she knew was a vampire.

If they had a chance of staying together, he must give her that same trust. So he unfastened the snap at the top of his jeans. She helped him, lowering his zipper and reaching inside to clasp his erection in her hand.

"That feels wonderful," she whispered.

He laughed. "At this end, too."

They were both unsteady on their feet now. And he helped her down to the carpet where she stretched the length of her body against his.

"Nick, make love with me," she whispered.

He was helpless to deny her. To deny himself what he had been craving since the last time, when he hadn't allowed himself fulfillment.

He wanted her hot and ready for him—and she was. He knew why he was postponing their joining. He didn't know how it would end.

He stroked her breasts, then slid his hand downward to her most intimate flesh to find her wet and swollen. And when he touched her, her hips moved in response to the stroking of his fingers. Every ounce of his attention was tuned to her, to the tiny sounds she made and the ripples of sensation that flowed across her body as he gave her pleasure.

Her voice turned urgent. "Nick, I want you inside me."

He would have held back, but she clasped him in her hand, squeezing and stroking him, making it impossible for him to wait any longer.

He covered her body with his, plunging into her with a steady stroke. Her eyes were open, her gaze locked with his as he began to move.

She called his name again, moving with him, driving toward completion. He felt her inner muscles contract, felt her take him to the very edge of climax. He might still have lost his nerve and done what he did the last time, denied himself complete fulfillment, even though his fang sheaths were throbbing with need. But she cupped her hands around the back of his head and pressed his mouth to her shoulder.

"Do it," she murmured.

He groaned, not knowing if he were about to have his worst fears or his fondest dreams realized. He gave her soft skin a tender kiss. Then, surrendering himself to her and to his nature, he sank his fangs into her neck.

Emma made a small sound, and an agony of uncertainty tore at him. She was in pain, and instinctively he reached out with his mind to ease it.

"Don't," she gasped out. "Don't take this part of it away from me."

With a terrible effort, he drew back the curtain, allowing her to remain aware as he drank the sweet blood that poured into his mouth while a powerful orgasm ripped through his body. When the orgasm was over, it was hard to stop drinking. But he knew he must, if he wanted to keep her safe. So he took only a little. Just enough to complete the act for him. And then, tenderly, he used his tongue to seal the small punctures he had made.

When he pulled back, she gasped his name. Turning his head away, he wiped his mouth on the back of his hand, then cradled her close, his anxious gaze focused on her face.

"Emma?" he managed to ask. "Did I hurt you?"

"Only a little."

"I'm so sorry."

She stroked his shoulder. "Don't be. I felt your pleasure when you drank. Thank you for sharing that with me."

Overwhelmed, he felt tears gather in his eyes, and he hugged her to himself as a wave of profound relief washed over him.

"Was that the way you want it to be?" she asked.

"Oh, yes." He kissed her lips, then her cheek. "But I was sure you'd want to run away."

"I know. That's why I didn't give you a chance for second thoughts."

"We haven't solved all our problems," he forced himself to say.

"Right. You're not going to get older, and I will. And we both know there's only one long-term solution to that problem."

He felt his body stiffen and his heart start to pound.

"I'm…considering letting you make me a vampire," she said.

A moment of silence passed.

"It's not a risk-free procedure," he said, his voice rough and not quite steady.

"I know. I read about it in your books. But Thorn said—"

"Bloody hell, you talked to him about that, too?"

"Yes, and he said his research team ought to be able to find a way to make it safer."

Drawing back a little, he met her gaze. "And you'd do it? Let me change you?"

Her gaze didn't waver from his as she nodded. "I want to think about it more, but I think so. Don't make me decide tonight."

"Of course not." No, he wouldn't rush her— even though his own impulse was to leap up with her in his arms and dance, laughing with joy. He could hardly believe this was real. It seemed more like a dream, as if they had, indeed, stepped back into the dream where they'd first met.

But her smile was real, and the feel of her naked body pressed against his was very real. He didn't know if he could bear the happiness that filled him.

"I won't rush you," he said, his lips brushing her temple. "To begin with, I know you'll need to think about your sister and how you'd handle your relationship with her."

"Yes," Emma agreed. "But once she's back on her feet again—back to her steady, sober self, I think she'll be relieved to see me settled in a stable relationship."

"You wouldn't be able to tell her what you were—or what I am."

She sat up and huffed out a breath. "For pity's sake, Nick, we can't figure out everything in one night!"

He grinned. "You're right. But may I suggest that we might be more comfortable discussing the matter in a bed."

"Yes."

He went down to one of the staterooms with her, and they settled into the wide berth, where they talked for a long time about the past few days and the future.

Finally, he said, "It's getting late. I have to get back inside the office."

She pointed to one of the portholes. "I had blackout shades installed."

"You knew I'd come here?"

"I hoped."

He relaxed back against the pillows, his admiring gaze following her nude form as she got up and pulled the blinds, fastening them to the bulkhead with snaps, shutting the room away from the world.

Then she turned on the bedside lamp and opened the drawer next to her side of the berth. Pulling out a small box, she handed it to him.

When he lifted the lid, his breath caught. Inside were two silver rings with a bold Celtic pattern worked into the surface.

"They're beautiful. You made them?"

"Yes. I've been spending my time in the silversmith workshop, when I wasn't reading. Working was a way to steady myself, and then I realized I wanted to make these rings."

She lifted up the larger ring and held it out, and he slipped it on his finger. He did the same for her with the smaller ring.

Contentment and the sunrise made his voice drowsy as he said, "You were taking a chance, weren't you, making rings for us?"

She smiled, a sultry woman's smile. "I hoped I could...persuade you to my way of thinking. I hope you like them."

"I love them." Against his will, he felt his eyelids drifting closed.

"Sleep," she murmured. "I'll be here when you wake up."

# HARLEQUIN®
# INTRIGUE®

## WE'LL LEAVE YOU BREATHLESS!

If you've been looking for thrilling tales of
contemporary passion and sensuous love stories
with taut, edge-of-the-seat suspense—then
you'll love Harlequin Intrigue!

Every month, you'll meet six new heroes
who are guaranteed to make your spine tingle
and your pulse pound. With them you'll enter
into the exciting world of Harlequin Intrigue—
where your life is on the line
and so is your heart!

## THAT'S INTRIGUE—
## ROMANTIC SUSPENSE
## AT ITS BEST!

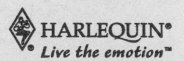

HARLEQUIN®
*Live the emotion*™

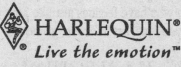

# HARLEQUIN®
## Presents~

**The world's bestselling romance series...**
**The series that brings you your favorite authors,**
**month after month:**

Helen Bianchin...Emma Darcy
Lynne Graham...Penny Jordan
Miranda Lee...Sandra Marton
Anne Mather...Carole Mortimer
Susan Napier...Michelle Reid

**and many more uniquely talented authors!**

Wealthy, powerful, gorgeous men...
Women who have feelings just like your own...
The stories you love, set in exotic, glamorous locations...

# HARLEQUIN®
## Presents~

**Seduction and Passion Guaranteed!**

## Harlequin Historicals®
### Historical Romantic Adventure!

*From rugged lawmen and valiant knights to defiant heiresses and spirited frontierswomen, Harlequin Historicals will capture your imagination with their dramatic scope, passion and adventure.*

*Harlequin Historicals . . . they're too good to miss!*

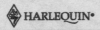
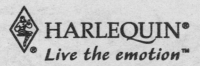